THE HOUSE UP DOC POLLY HOLLER

J.F. COMBS

authorHOUSE®

AuthorHouse™
1663 Liberty Drive
Bloomington, IN 47403
www.authorhouse.com
Phone: 833-262-8899

Published by AuthorHouse 05/06/2021

ISBN: 978-1-6655-2502-2 (sc)
ISBN: 978-1-6655-2500-8 (hc)
ISBN: 978-1-6655-2501-5 (e)

Library of Congress Control Number: 2021909402

Print information available on the last page.

Any people depicted in stock imagery provided by Getty Images are models,
and such images are being used for illustrative purposes only.
Certain stock imagery © Getty Images.

This book is printed on acid-free paper.

Because of the dynamic nature of the Internet, any web addresses or links contained in
this book may have changed since publication and may no longer be valid. The views
expressed in this work are solely those of the author and do not necessarily reflect the
views of the publisher, and the publisher hereby disclaims any responsibility for them.

CONTENTS

CHAPTER ONE

It was November 13, 1969. The three of us were taking a walk and stumbled upon an old abandoned house up Doc Polly Holler in Madison, West Virginia. It was a cold day, but we didn't mind because we were twenty years old without a care in the world.

Annabelle with her long golden blonde hair, that flowed behind her as she sprinted along stood about 5'5", was very outgoing with a bubbling personality. Linda was 6'1" with long brown hair that bounced as she walked along side me. She was always hesitant about going into crowed spaces, but she was very smart. I, September, like my favorite month and a nickname given to me by my mom, was 5'2" with short red hair that lay in curls just at my shoulders. I loved exploring and always looked for a new adventure. Annabelle was wearing jeans with holes, t-shirt, and boots. I had on coveralls and hiking boots, and Linda was wearing sweatpants, a sweatshirt, and tennis shoes.

We followed the winding road, stepping over dead tree roots, the dry leaves crunching beneath our shoes. The rain fell gently as we sang, our voices echoing through the trees that seemed to be intertwined with each other, standing strong. A brisk wind was blowing as if warning us of an upcoming storm, but we kept going. I love thunderstorms, but only in the summer.

We could hear the animals going about their way, and even saw some playing around as we proceeded further up the holler. We had gone about four miles when in the distance, we saw an old, abandoned house. The sidewalk leading to the house was broken, and the long, unkept grass was reaching across the concrete as if it were hugging in the quietness.

The steps leading up to the porch were crooked and narrow, with only a plank of rotten wood used for a railing, which several crows were perched upon, cawing softly.

The weathered porch showed signs of rot, and the house's white painted clapboard siding was streaked by the drainage of the leaky tin gutter that ran along the rusty roof that bowed in the center. Ivy crawled up the house, almost reaching the lengthy windows covered with torn plastic that were unable to withstand the elements. The door hung on hinges that had seen too much rain, and slightly ajar, the windowsills were blistered from the sun.

Sounds of scrapping, howling, and panting filled the air as we walked through the long grass, leaving behind just our footprints in the dew. We weren't really used to the strange wilderness, but we were bored stiff. Annabelle was wanting to go deeper into the holler, but Linda and I didn't.

The house sat on a knoll overlooking a valley where lots of trees stood tall and adorned the property. Tied to one of the huge sycamores was a tire swing, and several feet away stood a dark blue playhouse, its features trimmed in light blue. Two names were written on the door, Hector and Luke, and a DO NOT ENTER sign hung just above. We tested the door, jiggling the doorknob, and it was unlocked, so we went inside.

The walls were painted blue, and the space was decorated with homemade curtains, a child's table with 2 chairs, and scattered cushions and blankets. Small shelves adorning the walls held matchbox cars. A chalkboard hanging on the wall looked to have been written on frequently. We walked around to the back of the house and saw a creek, its water flowing across rocks as it wound its way around debris. It was so peaceful watching the water run and fish coming up to the surface. A narrow old bridge stretched across the creek with ropes to cling to as you walked across, its boards loose from years of use. On the other end of the bridge, we could see fallen trees, a broken-down picnic table, rusted-out motorcycle, and some trash.

We noticed there was a deck that looked sturdy but weathered, with cinderblocks used for steps. The back door was weathered, its paint curled with age, and a dirty worn-out rug lay in front of the door. Sitting on the deck were two old yellow metal motel armchairs, and a Maytag wringer washer sat off to the left, appearing like it had washed its last load of clothes. We were in awe because we hadn't seen anything like this, except maybe at our grandparents' house. To the right of the deck was a white doghouse with a metal roof, hidden in the long grass, a rubber flap nailed in front of the opening to keep out the harsh elements.

We stood there wondering whether we should go in. Anxiety crept over me as we stood there just listening in the silence, when suddenly a mighty flash of lightning blanketed everything at once. Moments later there came rumbling thunder, and right on cue the rain began to fall haphazardly from the sky, as if it wasn't entirely committed to the idea of raining. Then all at once it fell in great sheets, and there was only one place for us to find shelter — in the house.

But before we could decide if we should go inside, another flash was followed by another angry sound of thunder. We were drenched but too scared to go inside.

Linda, squeezing the water out of her hair and shivering from the cold said, "I saw a building over by the broken picnic table in the woods."

"Let's go there," Annabelle said, tears running down her rosy wet cheeks, her voice quavering from the cold. "The wind is cutting through the holes in my jeans like a knife," she continued. I felt bad that I brought them here and that they might get sick or hurt. The three of us had been friends for a long time, and I couldn't handle it if something happened to them. We had taken many walks before, but never up a holler.

3

CHAPTER TWO

Boom! Another loud crack of thunder sent us running, leaving only our shoeprints behind as our shoes squished in the mud. As we crossed the bridge, it wobbled back and forth like a duck, but we crossed anyway, determined to get inside the building.

The rain was still coming down in sheets, and the water was rising fast. We feared the rising water because lots of flooding has occurred in these parts of West Virginia.

"This way, hurry," I told them, but after we reached the building, we saw the door had a padlock. "Don't look like we're going in there unless we can pry the lock off," I continued, while jumping up and down, about to pee my pants. "Come on, we have to go in the house or we will get pneumonia," I pleaded. "Or you can stand out here and I'll go back to the house and go inside."

Standing in the pouring rain like three dumb asses, trying to decide what to do, Annabelle suddenly started banging the lock with her boot. The lock was rusty, so after a couple of hits; the lock hit the ground. We quickly ran inside but left the door open so we could watch the rising water. Linda spotted an old bucket for us to pee in, as I had been holding mine for quite a while. We were getting hungry and our bellies were rumbling, so we discussed the idea of going back to the old house because it didn't look like the rain would stop any time soon.

We could hear noises, sounds that would make your skin crawl and your teeth chatter, coming from the woods. I thought the noise was coming from the house, but realized it was coming from behind the building.

"Hell no, I am out of here," I screamed, my heart racing as fast as a cheetah. By the time I turned around, Linda and Annabelle were already across the bridge. The noises were loud and seemed to be getting closer; it sounded like an animal growling.

Thinking it was a panther, I picked up my pace and ran like a bat out of hell trying to catch up with the others.

As I reached the house, Linda was shaking like leaves on a tree, jogging in place to get warm. Annabelle was just standing there freezing, her arms crossed as she stared at the door.

"Well, anyone want to go in now?" I asked, feeling frustrated and scared. Not waiting for a response, I stretched out my trembling hand and pushed the door open slowly. As the door scraped across the wooden floor, we stepped inside. My heart felt as though it was going to stop beating. We were shivering to the bone, so we hoped to find heat and dry clothes. As we stood in the foyer, our feet felt as though they were frozen in place, and water dripped from our clothes to form puddles on the floor. We listened quietly for any sounds hiding inside the old house but heard only our heartbeats.

We held hands and proceeded further. To the left of the door was a beat-up desk, a vase of red dried roses atop of it. The drawers were squeaky and rickety as we opened the, finding crayons, coloring books, and a couple of puzzles inside. Beside the desk was a larger round pedestal table with 6 chairs. We then walked across the squeaky floor over to an old trunk sitting in the middle of the living room. The trunk was made of pine wood painted orange and had a dome top covered with children's stickers, like The Incredible Hulk, Hot Wheels, some Ram Doss white stickers, and Tops Wacky Sticker Cards.

Everything looked old like at my grandma's house.

Under the trunk was a handmade oval braided rug made of wool.

Some of the threads were unraveling and it didn't appear to have been cleaned for a long time. Directly across from the front door was a fireplace; the mantle was oak with dark stain, and it was shockingly huge, and the ashes hadn't been cleaned out. A set of fireplace tools was sitting to the right on the hearth. Hanging above the mantle was a cuckoo clock, that looked like a small cottage with hand-carved bears and trees.

To the right of the room sitting catty-corner was an orange upholstered couch with rolled arms, its cushions dirty and torn. A small and round table sat next to the couch, held up by a center leg and three clawed feet. It held an amber glass lamp with a white shade. Under the table was a cardboard box covered with cobwebs. As darkness was falling, we tried the light switch, but no electric.

"We need to find flashlights," Linda whispered. We crept over to the box, pulled it out and opened the flaps to look inside. Inside we found batteries, flashlights, old black and white pictures, mostly family photos and two handguns and shells. We were so thankful that we found guns and shells in case we needed to protect ourselves.

We gathered all the items that we needed except the photos, because they wouldn't help us in any way, and slowly walked to the sticker covered trunk and knelt in front of it. The hinges on the trunk were rusty, but when Annabelle reached her unsteady hand out to lift up the top, it was locked.

"Wonder where the damn key is…" Annabelle said loudly.

"Shh," I whispered, as she jumped to her feet and crossed her arms, perturbed.

"Calm the hell down, Annabelle," Linda told her, then jumped to her feet.

"We need to find dry clothes," I said. I was going to suggest we spread out and look for the key, but I knew they wouldn't go for that—we were all too scared. As I looked into their eyes, I knew what they were going to say.

"Hell no, we're not splitting up," Annabelle declared. "I would rather eat porcupines.

I laughed as my belly jiggled like a bowl of jelly.

"Well, I guess we will have to wear wet clothes then," I said with my usual attitude. *I can be stubborn too*, I thought to myself. The wet clothes were causing me to itch like crazy. As they stood there discussing what to do, I politely walked over to the couch, plopped my wet body down, and let the cushion hug my ass. I was going to have to give them a chance to figure things out on their own.

Linda suddenly shouted, "Let's just go together." I rose to my feet and joined them to the kitchen to begin our search.

CHAPTER THREE

As we entered the kitchen, there was a food pantry just to the right. We peeked inside and saw some canned goods like Vienna sausage, corn, green beans, peas, canned apples, soup, and several other cans with missing labels. The kitchen was small, about 10ft x 10ft, and the cabinets were painted white. Two cabinet doors were missing, and one drawer by the sink was left open exposing its contents. I searched the open drawer and found more flashlights, batteries, several boxes of kitchen matches, and glue.

The porcelain sink had no faucet and was sat below a small window with just a white cotton swag. The stove and refrigerator were green, complementing the blue walls. The blue vinyl flooring was in a square pattern, though it was worn and chipped.

Linda opened the refrigerator but it was empty. On the refrigerator was a note, held in place with a magnet in the shape of a small saucepan. The note was dated August 1, 1969. It simply said — GONE EXPLORING.

Annabelle yelled, "Come here guys!"

Suddenly… *Click!*

"Holy shit, what was that?" I asked, my lips quivering from fear.

Without thinking, we ran and hid behind the couch, my heart now beating rapidly. We hid and watched for what felt like an hour, but saw nothing. I crawled over to the box where we found the guns and took another look. Taped under the box was a key. I removed it from the sticky tape, and with key in hand, I crawled back behind the couch where Annabelle and Linda were waiting anxiously.

"I found it," I said nervously.

Hesitantly, we crawled over to the trunk. I reached my trembling hand out and inserted the key and turned it slowly, hoping it wouldn't break. Not realizing I was holding my breath; I became dizzy and fainted.

"You okay, September?" Linda asked, rubbing my back.

"Yes," I spoke softly, coming to. "I'm okay. Now who's going to open it?"

The silence was deafening as Linda said with assurance, "I will." She stretched her shaky hand out toward the trunk and lifted the top slowly as the hinges squeaked, then yanked her hand back like she had touched fire.

We looked inside. *Clothes, finally,* I thought to myself. I just hoped some of them would fit us. We began to toss clothes out onto the floor and grabbed what we thought would fit us. Each of us picked out a top and a pair of pants. With a deep sigh of relief, we stripped naked and put the clothes on and thankfully they fit us; although they weren't a perfect fit, they were dry at least. As we continued to investigate, I noticed what looked like a worn-out notebook hidden beneath the pile of clothing.

"Look!" I said with excitement.

We wanted to know what was inside so bad, but decided we would read it after we looked around some more. I carefully placed the notebook on top of the desk, hoping not to rip it. We were ready to see what was upstairs. As we proceeded to the steps, the floor under our feet creaked with every step.

"Who's going first?" Annabelle asked.

"Linda, you go first," I murmured, because I knew she wouldn't.

"No," she answered quickly. As I raised my foot onto the first step, it went through the rotted wood.

"Are you okay?" Linda asked.

"Yes, I just twisted my ankle."

Linda pushed me aside and pulled her hair into a ponytail. "I'll go first."

As she bound up the creaky steps, I saw a spider in a web that was already full of bugs, just between two of the railings, so I moved to the other side of the steps. Linda reached the top quickly and we made our way up and stood beside her.

"Now what?" Annabelle asked, as she stooped over to tie her boots.

"Keep going," I said.

As we made our way down the dark hall, our breathing became loud, our hearts beating fast. There was a door on the left and two doors on the right, so we decided to enter the door on the left first. The door was white and had a glass doorknob. My hands were shaking as I reached and turned the knob, slowly pushing the door open. As we stepped inside, we were shocked to find a small child's room. Posters about exploring the universe and cartoons covered the walls, and stars were dangling from the ceiling.

A set of bunkbeds was against the wall just to the left. They were covered with Spider-Man blankets and the windows were covered with matching curtains.

Next to the beds was a small square table, a lamp with a Spider-Man shade sitting on top, and a basket of toys sat undisturbed on the floor next to the table. We then left that room and crossed the hall to another door. An eerie feeling overwhelmed me.

"Well go on in," Linda whispered.

Annabelle, wringing her hands nervously, reached out with an unsteady hand and opened the door.

"Thank God," I said, "a bathroom."

Annabelle and Linda were relieved as they too had been holding their pee. To the left was a small white vanity sink with two doors. To the right was a white, grimy toilet, and beside it was a claw foot tub filled with dirty clothes. The kitchen faucet was missing and we were thirsty, so I turned the bathroom faucet on and the water gurgled as it ran. We put our hands together to form a cup and we each got a drink. I found some cleaning supplies under the sink, and next to the commode was a small trashcan with a commode brush. Towels and washcloths lie neatly stacked on the back of the commode.

"I have to pee now," Annabelle said, squeezing her thighs together, hoping it would not run down her legs and into her only boots. We cleaned the commode and took turns peeing, but no toilet paper was found. Feeling relieved but still nervous, we exited the bathroom and walked to the other door, the floors screeched with each step. Curious about what we would find next, but feeling a little more courageous, I reached out and opened the last door upstairs. The room was enormous. Straight ahead was a large brown metal bed, made up neatly with a handmade double wedding ring patchwork quilt, and a small table sat next to the bed, covered with a doily. On top of it was a small round alarm clock, and a small locket dangled from the edge.

To the right under a drape-covered window was what looked to be an antique dresser with a small bench in front of it. We were shocked to see a white crib up against the left wall. It was adorable with a Holly Hobbies quilt, and stuffed animals sitting around the railings of the crib keeping watch.

Startled by the *Click!* of a gun, we tried to run, but it felt as though our feet were stuck, frozen with fear. Suddenly, Annabelle hit the floor. She had fallen in shock.

"Come on, we have to help her," I cried. Our hearts were pounding out of our chests, now realizing we weren't alone anymore.

We couldn't run, so we dragged Annabelle under the bed with us. We silenced our breathing as best as we could. A beam of light was moving down the hallway past the room where we were hiding.

Annabelle was waking up and began to talk. "What the hell is going on?" she screamed loudly.

"Shh," I whispered, "they will find us."

After hiding for about an hour, not hearing any noises or seeing anyone, we crawled out from under the bed quietly and rose to our feet. We took deep breaths and sighed with relief that we weren't found and walked out the door and down the hallway. With no more doors to open upstairs, we proceeded back down the steps quickly, but quietly.

CHAPTER FOUR

"I'm hungry," I told them, and Annabelle and Linda said they were too. I could hear their stomachs rumbling. Linda headed to the other room and made us a fire while Annabelle and I gathered food from the pantry. Annabelle, feeling better now, opened the door to the pantry and grabbed some Vienna sausages and I grabbed some plastic forks from the opened drawer. It was getting dark, so we got our flashlights out and pushed the trunk off the braided rug and sat down to eat because it was closer to the fireplace.

While eating, I remembered the notebook we had found. We were all eager to learn what was hidden within it. I stood up and quietly walked across the squeaky floor to get the notebook and returned to where the others were. I gently opened the notebook, careful not to rip its pages.

As Linda held the flashlight on the page, I began to read its content. The first page was dated July 28, 1969. It read: *I awoke to a strange clicking noise tonight, like the sound of a loading gun outside the window. I immediately gathered my family and brought them to the living room where we could all be in front of the fire for warmth. Nora was frantic as we sat there, she was holding onto Lilly, our baby girl, like someone was trying to pry her out of her arms. My six-year-old son Hector was too fearful to get off my lap and my 11-year-old son Luke was sitting on the floor in front of us. I have my gun loaded and ready should I need to protect us. The doors are locked and boarded, we should be safe here.* It was signed, *Bubba.*

I think we have an unsolved crime on our hands. I gently closed the book and suggested to the other two girls that we needed to be extremely careful because something strange had happened here. Linda stood and stretched and then walked over to the window and pulled the curtain over a little, peeking outside.

"See anything?" Annabelle asked.

"It's snowing," Linda said.

"Did anyone see any blankets?" I asked. "I'm freezing my ass off."

"I'm up, I'll get some," Linda said. She was alluding to the stack of blankets neatly folded on the floor by the couch. She closed the curtains and tiptoed to the couch, picking up the blankets.

Click!

"Did you all hear that?" Linda asked fearfully, running to us.

Again, *click!* We all heard it and hid under the cover, hoping it would hide us.

"I think the noise came from outside," Annabelle inferred. We sat still and quiet for a while until we felt safe.

"Anybody thirsty?" I asked. "I'll get some glasses and then you two can go get some water from upstairs."

"Who died and made you the boss?" Annabelle asked snarly.

"I brought us here and that makes me the boss," I said. Then I walked across the squeaky floor and into the kitchen. I reached up, having to stand on my toes, and got 3 glasses from the top cabinet and took them to Linda and Annabelle. Linda and Annabelle, now annoyed at me, stomped off toward the steps while I headed towards the living room to tend to the fire.

Click! The sound seemed to be a little closer. I immediately dashed into the hall closest and left a small gap in the door so I could see what or who was making that sound. I could hear Linda and Annabelle discussing how her boots were causing a blister. Annabelle told Linda to go on up the stairs, so I don't think they heard the noise this time. My concern for them grew. I opened the closet door and looked around, but didn't see anyone.

I tread softly and as quiet as possible, hoping the floor wouldn't creak beneath my feet, and walked towards the stairs. As I lifted my foot, I tripped over a square-shaped dirty braided rug that lay at the foot of the stairs. My foot, already sprained, began to swell and the pain was relentless. At last, they came springing down the steps.

"Did you all not here that clicking noise?" I inquired.

"No? And what happened to you?" Linda asked, seemingly concerned.

"I tripped over that damn rug and hurt my sore foot." I moaned in pain. "I heard that clicking noise again," I told them as they helped me back to the living room and they sat next to me where Annabelle handed me a glass of water. My lips and tongue were very dry, so I drank it with one big gulp. My ankle was swollen but we had no ice. Linda stood back up and made a bandage from a shirt and wrapped it tightly around my ankle.

"That feels better," I said, letting out a sigh of relief. "Hand me the notebook, but please be careful." As soon as Annabelle picked up the notebook and sat back down, a loud scraping sound was coming from just outside the house.

"Was that the noise you heard September?" Linda asked, her lips quivering.

"No," I replied, "I heard that clicking noise that we heard upstairs." My heart felt as though it was going to jump out of my chest, it was beating so fast.

Annabelle had pulled the blanket up over her head, and I could see her chest moving up and down through the cover. As the sound got louder, we all got under the cover. After we calmed down a little and didn't hear anything, we decided to go see what it was and where it was coming from.

CHAPTER FIVE

was in some serious pain, but I knew they wouldn't go without me. I tried to stand, but it was difficult, so they helped me to my feet.

"Get one of the guns, Linda, and make sure it's loaded. Annabelle, get the poker over by the fireplace," I instructed.

We picked up our flashlights, and with weapons in hand, walked to the front door. I was so nervous and I sensed that they were too because they were trembling. Linda's hand was trembling as she reached for the doorknob. She turned the knob hesitantly and pulled, the door scraping the floor as it opened. Annabelle raised the poker as we stepped onto the porch. Shining my light through the darkness, I saw nothing at first, but a suppressed scream vibrated in my throat as I spotted a car off in the distance, partially hidden by some trees. We walked down the rotted steps and proceeded towards the car.

The snow was still falling and it blanketed the ground, but we continued slowly as we left behind our footprints in the snow. I was going to check out the building again while they checked out the car.

"I need the poker; will you trade me please Annabelle?" I asked. I wasn't quite ready for a gun, so we exchanged weapons, then I turn round slowly, and with a limp, walked towards the back of the house. It was dark and freezing, and my flashlight was flickering. As I began to walk across the narrow bridge, I saw bloody paw prints in the snow.

As I approached the building and moved my light through the

darkness, I saw a dark form at the edge of the tree line. The padlock had been broken off and sat at my feet on the ground.

I took several deep breaths and pushed the door open and listened as it dragged across the dirt floor. After seeing the shadow, I quickly stepped inside. I moved my light around in the dark building, finding big wheels, bicycles, stuffed animals, and other toys.

Parked in the middle was an old rusty tractor, appearing to have sat there for quite a while. As I looked further, I saw a cardboard box covered in dust sitting on the seat of the tractor. Feeling curious, I picked up the box and placed it down on the dirt floor and sat next to it so I could take a peek inside.

My ankle was hurting and I was very tired. My mind kept wandering back to Annabelle and Linda, hoping they were safe. I blew some of the dust off the box and raised the flaps. I pulled out a birthday card and wept as I began to read: *Happy First Birthday Lilly! Love always, Dad.* Tears ran down my red, cold cheeks, and my eyes were getting heavy. I couldn't stop yawning, so I drifted off to sleep.

I was jolted awake by someone or something shaking me, I could feel their cold touch on my shoulders. I briskly rose to my feet and started kicking, punching, and scratching, at whatever touched me, when I heard a soft whisper.

"Calm down September, it's me! Linda. I can't find Annabelle," she cried frantically. I sat back down and patted the ground beside me signaling her to sit beside me. She was so upset, but she laid her head on my shoulders, and finally calmed down. I then noticed her staring under the tractor.

"What is it, Linda?" I asked. She just pointed to the tractor, and all I could hear was the word 'blood'. I shined my light under the tractor, and saw a stuffed animal - a lamb - with what looked like blood on it. It seemed to be half buried and next to it was a pack of cigarettes.

"We have a crime to solve now more than ever," I said to myself, and wondered what in the hell had happened here?

I continued looking through the box and just after moving over a piece of clothing, I saw a knife wrapped in a piece of leather. After unwrapping it, I saw that the blade was covered in a red stain also. I tucked the knife in the back of my pants, just in case I would need it.

"Oh Lord! What are we going to uncover?" I asked myself out loud. I also found a pair of stiff leather gloves, and they too were covered in red stains. Linda, now feeling safe, started telling me a shocking story about a guy she used to date named Donnie.

"Well," she began, "he disappeared around June 6, 1969; he was last seen at a Dairy Queen in Madison, West Virginia, wearing a red plaid shirt, red ballcap, white tennis shoes and jeans."

I listened intently to what she was going to say next. Then she continued, "His car was also missing from the Dairy Queen parking lot. That same night, a fourteen-year-old girl came up missing from a nearby gas station, her name was Misty."

As I listened closely, I was curious about why she hadn't mentioned this to me before. It was told around town that Donnie liked young girls. She said, "He was twenty-three years old and was a hunter, so he knew the woods."

"Did you and Annabelle make it to the parked car?" I asked.

"No," she replied, "she took off in another direction. I just assumed she was behind me, but when I turned around to ask her a question, she was gone.

I couldn't help but wonder if Donnie was out here in this holler and took Annabelle. Then I heard snoring.

Linda had fallen asleep with her head on my shoulder and her long hair was covering her round face. My mind was on what Linda had just told me, and the mystery we had stumbled upon.

I frantically scrambled to my feet after I heard a loud gunshot in the woods, not far from the building. It startled us, and as soon as I jumped to my feet, she jumped up.

"What the hell September?" she yelled.

"Shut up stupid, there was a gunshot out back," I told her, hostility in my voice. "We have to get the hell out of here now Linda," I demanded. But she sat there fiddling with her hair, like always.

"Well, I'm going back to the house," I said. I was now getting furious with her. "Get up Linda we must go now." She seemed to get her faculties together finally, and we quietly but quickly walked to the front of the building.

"Coast is clear, run now!" I advised after I stuck my head out the door and looked all around. I was so scared we would get shot. Not giving a thought about my sore ankle, I ran like a bat out of hell, hoping Linda was behind me. My heart was racing as I reached the porch. I looked behind me only to see Linda as she zoomed past me and hurried into the house. I stepped inside quickly and shut the door behind me and locked it.

"Thank you, September," Linda said softly, hugging me tightly.

We waited for a moment to catch our breath before deciding to look for Annabelle before complete darkness fell. We unlocked the door hesitantly and wandered down the steps, following the broken sidewalk in search for clues. Linda stopped abruptly and stooped over, picking up a silver chain with a camo locket dangling from it.

"Wasn't that upstairs on the bed side table?" I asked.

"Yes," she replied.

She then opened it up and inside was a photo of a family. A man, a woman, and three kids, just like Bubba had described in the notebook. *Could this be them?* I thought to myself.

"Annabelle must have taken it," Linda suggested.

We decided to head to the car. The car was covered in mud and appeared to be sunken into the ground. With my coat sleeve, I wiped the window so I could take a peek inside. The key was still in the ignition, which was very strange. I pulled on the door handle and to my surprise, it opened. Linda immediately saw a red plaid shirt hanging on the back of the driver's seat.

"This is Donnie's shirt and car," she assured me, trembling. She had told me that someone had beat her once, and I bet it was Donnie. "We need to find Annabelle," Linda said impatiently.

"Oh, Linda you know Annabelle, she's probably pulling a trick on us. Let's just keep investigating," I said.

"Ok, she said in a loud voice, if something happens to her, I'll blame you September."

"Whatever Linda," I yelled angrily. Out of the corner of my eye, I could see weeds shuffling, and it startled me. Overwhelmed with fear, Linda squatted down in the floorboard.

"Come on let's get this investigation going. It's probably Annabelle being her crazy self. Look it's just a deer," I told her.

"Are you sure?" she asked with trembling lips.

"Yes, I'm sure. Get up and look," I said. She slowly raised herself back into the seat. While looking around further inside the car, Linda suddenly screamed.

"Oh my God! There's a backpack in the backseat."

I slid out of the driver's seat and opened the back door so I could see the contents of the bag, hoping it would reveal who it belonged to.

"Oh no this isn't good," I heard. Linda was now behind me peering around me, to see what I find inside.

"When did Donnie and Misty go missing?" I asked.

"June or July of this year."

"Holy shit! That's around the same date on the note we found on the refrigerator," I noted.

The backpack had a team logo of Jan Sport on it. Some of its contents had fallen out, and were strewn across the floorboard including several spiral notebooks, that were colorful and labeled very neatly. Trying not to disturb anything, I carefully searched inside the backpack. All I saw inside were shorts and a t-shirt. I shut the door back and got back into the driver's seat. Laying on the dashboard was a hairbrush, and in the passenger seat floorboard, there was a few dirty clothes.

"He took her," Linda yelled angrily.

"What have we stumbled upon?" I asked. "I fear for our lives now more than ever," I mumbled quietly. Linda was already freaked out and I didn't want to make it worse.

Then, Linda got out of the car and came over to the driver's side, reached in, and popped the trunk. But before I could say no, the trunk was up. I got out of the car and cautiously joined her at the back of the car, concerned we'd find dead bodies in there.

Linda's mouth flew open wide before I could see the contents, but she couldn't speak; her words were silent as she tried to talk and her lips quivered.

"Linda," I cried. "What is it? What did you see?" I couldn't look inside, so I closed the trunk. We stood silent and all we could hear was the rustling of the leaves in now the gusty wind.

The fluttering leaves danced in the high boughs. Sounds of dead trees creaked at every push the wind gave. The seen and unseen birds were singing.

"Linda," I screamed, "we have to go." But she couldn't seem to move, so I grabbed her by her shirt tail and pulled her vigorously.

"Trunk," she murmured. As I started back toward the house dragging Linda, I heard a scuffing noise behind me. I immediately let go of her. After I saw who it was, I relaxed.

"Annabelle, you scared the hell out of me," I berated.

"I scared you? You looked like you were going to rip my head off!" Annabelle screamed.

Click!

The sound startled us all. I spun around and yelled "Run!" as a bullet whizzed by us like a cheetah chasing a gazelle. The sound was deafening as the bullet hit the car, barely missing us. We helped Linda to her feet and ran toward the old house as if we were being chased by the Devil himself.

"Must have been a deer hunter," Annabelle suggested with a quiver in her lips. I had forgotten about the pain in my foot, because at this point, my adrenaline had kicked in.

CHAPTER SIX

lick!

It seemed like something or someone was chasing us as we ran up the steps to the porch. "Quick, grab some firewood," I said, pushing open the door so hard it hit in the inside wall. We each grabbed a few logs and ran inside. "We have to bar the doors."

Quickly, we pushed the desk up to the front door and pushed the table in front of the back door.

"I'll close the curtains," Annabelle added.

"We need a fire. It's too damn cold in here," I said, shivering uncontrollably.

After ensuring the doors were secure, we proceeded to the fireplace and built ourselves a fire. We put our cold shaky hands out in front of the warm heat escaping from the dancing flames and perched ourselves down on the chairs to enjoy the crackling sound of the fire.

As we sat, I saw the notebook. Excited to learn more, I jumped up and grabbed it carefully then returned to my chair. Curious to find out what else was hidden inside the pages of the notebook, I carefully opened its cover and turned the page. They both leaned closer beside me so they could see as well.

It was dated August 21,1969 and read: *I got up early this morning and left everyone in bed before I had my coffee, to see if I could find the source of the clicking sound. I quietly opened the door hoping not to wake anyone and went down the steps and just looked around. I could hear coyote in the distance, and I heard birds chirping in the trees. I then walked behind the house and saw bloody boot prints heading in the direction of the bridge. The grass was smashed down so I thought the footprints were pretty recent – Signed, Bubba.* I turned the page, but it was blank. More concerned than ever, but I placed the notebook back where I found it.

"Anyone want to tell ghost stories?" I asked.

"I guess," Linda said.

We began to tell ghost stories, and when it was my turn, I was going to have some fun with them. So, I began… "One night, a young woman couldn't find her baby that she had left in the crib. She was frantic until she heard a faint cry in one of the bedrooms. Someone had moved the baby, she thought. But who? The next day she found the baby in the kitchen sink. She thought someone was pulling a prank on her, until ---BOO!" I yelled, and they jumped like they had seen a ghost. I couldn't help but laugh although I was scared.

"Why are you all so jumpy? What's wrong? You said it was my turn," I said. Boy, they were mad at me now. Suddenly, I spotted something out of the corner of my eye. Linda seemed concerned as she saw me jump up from the chair and head toward the steps that led upstairs. She was immediately by my side. Annabelle, combing her hair with her fingers, finally stood up and made her way over to us. The corner of the rug was turned up, exposing a small door hidden underneath.

"You must have tripped on it when you hurt your ankle," Linda explained, turning to me.

We crouched down in front of the small door and could feel air escaping, and the smell of dampness was awful. I rested my cheeks in the palm of my hands, with elbows on my knees, and prayed. "Lord help us to get home safe and sound." I was wishing we were home, but the snow was deep, and my ankle was sore and swollen. I knew there was no way I'd be able to make the 4-mile walk home.

"I'm hungry—" I started to say, but before I could finish my sentence,

Linda and Annabelle were on their way to the kitchen. They must have heard my stomach rumble. I sat in front of the fire chewing my nails and watched the dancing flames.

My mind wandered back to the trunk of the car, questioning where Annabelle had been, the toy under the old tractor, where the family was that lived here, and now what mystery lay beneath the small door. I began to sob and worried that we may never make it back home.

I could taste the salty tears as they ran down my cheeks and landed softly on my lips. I sobbed for a long time, only able to smile when Annabelle and Linda came back from the kitchen.

"Thank you, guys, so much," I said as they handed me a bowl of tuna and a cup of coffee. I was so hungry; "This is good guys," I said. We were pacing back and forth peeking out the window. The temperature was falling as hard pellets of snow rattled on the metal roof. The sky was a dark gray-white, and mounds of snow blanketed the ground. In the beautiful snow we saw more prints.

We knew we had to get more firewood, and we weren't going to separate, because it was too dangerous. Bundled up best we could, we walked across the squeaky floor toward the front door. We huddled around closely, dreading to open it. We slid the desk away from the door, and I reached out, unlocked it, then slowly turned the doorknob.

"I remembered seeing more wood on the other side of that rickety bridge out back," I said.

As we reached the bottom of the steps, we could see the prints in the snow more clearly — they were bloody pawprints. We followed the prints and they led us to the snow-covered bridge. We proceeded across the bridge in a single line, then through the trees until we reached a clearing.

As we were gathering the wood, we heard scraping noises, like something was trying to get out of a confinement of some sort. My muscles twitched like a current of electricity running through my body.

With firewood in hand, we immediately started running back toward the house and knew something was chasing us. As we picked up our pace, whatever was chasing us, picked up their pace.

We were relieved to reach the house, I pushed the door open and we ran inside. I slammed the door shut immediately, barely missing my fingers. We pushed the desk back in front of the door and tried to catch our breaths. Fierce, vicious scraping sounds vibrated through the door, causing us to jump back. We returned to the living room and put wood on the fire, praying that whatever was outside, didn't get in.

"Tea anyone?" Linda asked as she turned toward the kitchen.

"Yes," I replied through chattering teeth. Annabelle grabbed a blanket and wrapped it tightly around me and handed me a cup of tea. I sipped it slowly. The scratching on the outside was causing fear to clog my throat. Although I was cold, perspiration was running down my back underneath my shirt. We sat there with our guns and the knife, and the fire poker beside us.

"We need another gun, so we'll each have one," Linda mumbled under her breath. "There's one in the car trunk," Linda added, her voice trembling. After getting warmed up, we decided to trick whatever was scratching at the front door to leave so we could run to the car. Annabelle suggested using Vienna sausage and hurried off to get a can. After she returned, we got our weapons and flashlights and proceeded to the back door.

We slid the table over and I opened the can as Annabelle opened the door. We threw the sausages out onto the deck one at a time and made lots of noise to draw the creature out back.

After a few seconds, we could hear it running fast towards the back door. We slammed the door shut and ran to the front door, listening for a few minutes. When all was quiet, we barged through the front door and ran to the car as fast as lighting, jumping inside the car and locking the doors. Our breaths fogged up the windows it was so cold. We sat

30

quietly and looked all around, constantly wiping the condensation off the windows.

"Where did you disappear to, Annabelle?" I asked curiously.

"I got lost," she said.

"Seriously?" I asked jokingly, "and what did you see in the trunk Linda?" She didn't answer me. All of a sudden, Annabelle jumped out of the car and came to the driver's side door. She opened it and reached in, pulling the trunk lever. The trunk went up and I watched her walk slowly to the back of the car. She grabbed the gun and shells and slammed the trunk back down.

Something must have frightened her because she ran back to the car visibly shaken, and jumped in and locked the door. I saw the same fear in her eyes as I saw in Linda's eyes after she had looked in the trunk.

"Let's get out of here," Annabelle said. "Try the key." She pointed to the key still in the ignition. I turned it a few times but the engine wouldn't start, likely from the cold, or perhaps the battery was dead.

Having no luck, we slouched back, defeated. "Shh, did you all hear that crackling noise? and can you smell the smoke?"

"No?" they answered simultaneously.

I looked up and the sky was blackened, ash landing on the car; it looked as if smoke was coming from the back of the house. Guns in hand, we jumped out of the car and headed for the back of the house, finding it was the building on fire. It was fully engulfed in flames as ash flew up into the heavens. We raced towards it, anxiously glancing around for the creature that had been trying to get into the house. With no sight of the creature, we stood and watched the building as it quickly became ashes and embers. The fire gave us heat, but the smoke was filling up our nostrils. Linda stood there gazing as her breath blew out in a cloud of steam, clapping her hands together to help regain her circulation.

"We better get back inside," I said, shaking uncontrollably. We dashed towards the house and ran inside, barricading the door behind us.

CHAPTER SEVEN

Annabelle put another log on the fire, then we sat back down in our chairs to warm ourselves up, feeling thankful it wasn't the house that burned down.

"Tea anyone?" I asked. Linda jumped up and went to the kitchen as she yelled, "Tea coming up." After Linda gave me my tea, I tasted it and was thrilled at the rich and sweet flavor.

"Thank you, Linda, the tea hit the spot and it was delicious." After I sipped my last drink, I asked if they wanted to go investigate what was under the small door hidden underneath the rug. The response was, "Hell yes of course!"

We, with weapons and flashlights in hand, got out of the chairs and walked across the squeaky floor to the small door. We all knelt down and I stretched my unsteady hand out, raising the hatch. The hinges were very rusty and creaked loudly. We used our lights to peer down, illuminating a set of narrow wooden steps. I picked up my gun — a shotgun — and headed backwards down the steps into the darkness.

"You guys follow me down slowly and don't knock me down," I said. When I reached the bottom, I could tell the floor was only dirt. I moved my light around and thought to myself that someone had been hiding down here. After they came down, we searched the room. It was a medium-sized space and one wall was covered in shelving.

A tall metal bed was up against the cinder block wall, and next to it was a small round glass top table with what looked like an oil lamp sitting on top. Beside it sat a small refrigerator, though after looking inside, we found it empty. A floor model television was sitting in the corner. I took the oil lamp from the table and examined it. The wick appeared to be in good shape but had very little oil.

"Anybody know where a lighter is?" I asked.

"I'll go upstairs and look," Annabelle answered quickly, "I remember seeing matches in the kitchen drawer." She went upstairs to get matches, while Linda and I sat on the bed and chatted, but my mind kept going back to the notebook. Annabelle returned a few minutes later and after a few tries at lighting the lamp, the room was lit brightly.

"Now we can get a good look as to what's on the shelves," I said excitedly.

And to our astonishment, the shelves were filled with goodies; a variety of canned goods, bottled water, instant coffee, creamer, a hand held can opener, two more lanterns, lamp oil, blankets and pillows, ammunition, and more flashlights and batteries. We now thought we could survive until the snow melted, but first we had to survive whoever was hiding out here.

We grabbed what we could and went back upstairs. After reaching the top, I slid the hatch back, covered it with the rug, and followed them to the kitchen where we set our goodies on the counter.

Linda asked us to tend to the fire and she would get us something to eat and drink. She then returned with soup and coffee. We started eating and made conversation between mouthfuls.

"What did you see in the trunk Linda?" I asked again.

Linda's spoon was shaking in her hand as she began to answer, her voice trembling, "A muddy shovel, bloody clothes, muddy boots, tarp, and blankets."

I tried to speak but my voice fell silent.

"You think the family that lived here is dead?" Annabelle asked.

"I don't know," I managed.

34

"Are you sure there weren't any more entries in the notebook?" Linda asked.

"No," I said softly, "but if you go get it, we can look."

When she handed me the notebook, I turned several pages before I saw another entry dated September 5, 1969. I began to read as the girls listened intently.

I noticed a car today coming out the holler, I knew we were the only family out here, so I ran back inside and immediately woke my family and demanded they go downstairs to the hidden room.

It's not often you see a vehicle out here this time of night. Sometimes in the daytime, someone would come out here simply because they were lost. After my family was safely down in the hidden room; I closed the door and concealed its existence with a rug. With my shotgun in hand, I quietly exited the house and hid behind some trees, careful not to be seen.

I watched closely as the door of the car opened, and a young man that appeared to be in his early twenties, exited the driver's side door wearing a red plaid shirt and ballcap. He walked to the trunk and opened it and dragged out a young girl, screaming and kicking.

I pointed my gun in that direction just in case they headed my way. My heart was pounding fast as I saw him drag her into the woods and out of sight. I couldn't help her because I had my family to protect. I would go out and call the police later, I thought. I was so afraid they would find us; I ran back inside and told my family to stay very quiet in case they came inside. Bubba.

We were becoming more fearful by the minute. My hands were shaking so bad that I dropped my coffee cup.

"We need to gather up everything we may need and hide it behind the couch so we can stay together," I told them, my heart pounding loudly.

We split from each other and gathered up everything we thought we would need; weapons, food, drink, pillows, blankets, flashlights, batteries, candles, and matches. We didn't know what was going on, but I saw the mystery unfolding before my eyes.

"We need to go and get the two-by-fours and nails and attach it across the door," I said.

So, Annabelle walked over to the door and stepped outside and got two pieces of board that we saw on the porch earlier. Linda handed me some nails and a hammer that were in the coffee can that we found in the hidden room. As soon as I nailed the board, a loud bang vibrated the door.

"Oh no, hurry! Nail the back door," Linda pleaded, "now!"

"I'm going as fast as I can, remember I have a sprained ankle?" I groused.

As the pounding continued and had gotten louder, we rushed to the back door and nailed a board across it. We all thought we were going to die here, and nobody would ever find us.

"Linda, Annabelle, go downstairs and hide, but be very quiet," I insisted. "Go now. I'm going to hide in the closet in case they break in. There are some gaps in the door, so maybe I can get a good look at them." They rushed around like chickens with their heads cut off.

"Come on guys please, I'm serious." So, with their hands filled, I helped them over to the steps, and down they went.

"I'll cover the door back up, don't make a sound. I'll let you know when it's safe to come back up," I explained. The girls were now safe, and the pounding got more forceful. I hurried into the closet that was close to the couch. I stood there like a statue made of stone. *I can't kill anyone,* I thought to myself. I was thinking that if we could survive the night, I would glue the rug down onto the door so we could all hide down there if we needed to.

CHAPTER EIGHT

could see light coming through the curtains and was hoping they would just go away.

Click!

Now thinking it was a gun, all I could do was pray, so I closed my eyes and prayed for God to protect us. After about thirty-minutes, it was eerily quiet. I couldn't help but wonder what they were up to. I pondered the fact that they might go to the back door and try breaking it down.

When I thought it was safe enough, I went over and peeked out the window. In the snow I could see fresh footprints leading to the car.

I went immediately to the hidden door and lifted it. I whispered and told them to come up and remain quiet and stay low. I gestured that I wanted something to drink and Linda nodded her head and proceeded to the kitchen.

We let the fire go out hoping no one would find out that we were here, then gathered up the blankets and sat next to Annabelle on the couch. Linda was tiptoeing towards us with drinks in her hands. We sat huddled together under the blankets and sipped our tea.

I quietly told them my plan to glue the rug onto the door, so if we needed to, we could all hide down there. They thought it was a good idea, so I went to the kitchen and got the glue from the drawer, then returned to the small door and lifted the rug, spreading the glue over the door. I replaced the rug and walked on it for a while to make sure it was flat, then went back to the couch and sat down. After our cups were empty, we placed them on the floor just under the couch because it had gotten a lot colder and we didn't want to get back up. Before we knew it, we were sound asleep.

Startled by a loud pounding on the back door, we jumped to our feet and felt around in the dark of night to find our weapons. Linda begged us to go downstairs.

We were all panicked as we could only see each other with our flashlights. The pounding got louder and it sounded as though they were now kicking the door. We knew it was a matter of time before they'd kick the door down and discover we were in here and kill us.

We grabbed what we could and quickly ran to the door and lifted it up and proceeded down the steps one after the other. I closed the door behind us and hoped the rug would cover the door back up and we would be safe, but I felt that we would die tonight. A loud clang hit the floor above us. I climbed to the top of the steps and instantly heard footsteps above me. My heart raced, and my legs were shaking, so I headed back down.

"They're inside," I whispered. The footsteps appeared like they were now moving upstairs.

"Do you think they know we're here?" Annabelle asked quietly.

"Hell yes," I said as I was tired of this shit. "They will die tonight if they find us," I promised.

It sounded like someone was taking a shower because we could hear the water running. *So, they must be familiar with this place,* I thought to myself. Linda was holding on to me tightly as the boards above us were creaking. I could barely speak as I fought to keep my voice steady. *What are we going to do now?* I questioned myself.

"Wait, did you all hear that?" I whispered.

Linda answered, her voice muffled, "Yes I did."

It sounded as though they were walking back down the stairs, their footsteps stopping on the rug above us. I quietly went back up the steps again, and heard shuffling. *Oh my God, please don't let them find us.* My stomach felt nauseous and it churned as I tried not to throw up.

Were they going to discover the door and come kill us? Annabelle and Linda were squirming around like a mouse stuck in a glue trap.

I aimed my gun up toward the door finding it hard to steady my aim as my arms were shaking and very unsteady. We ran to the bed and watched like sitting ducks, just waiting. Smoke began to seep through the cracks into the room, I covered my mouth and nose hoping not to cough or sneeze. My arm went limp and the gun fell down on the bed beside me. Annabelle grabbed it immediately and pointed it towards the stairs.

"No worries," she boasted, "I got this. Our hearts pounded loudly, adrenaline so high at this point, we could almost hear each other's thoughts.

"Under the bed now, hurry!" I urged them.

As we got in the right position, I could hear the hinges screech as the door creaked open. A foot was now on the top step as we cuffed our hands over our mouths again trying to suppress the sound of our breathing. My blood turned to slush as I prayed, *God please don't let them find us.* It was so cold down here and being nervous made it worse. As the figure reached the bottom step, we could see it was a man of about 22-23 years old. He was tall and thin, and his beard was long and bushy, as though he hadn't shaved for quite some time.

He was smoking a cigarette and blowing out circles of smoke. We could see the barrel of a gun and muddied boots as he stomped a cigarette onto the dirt floor, smothering it out. *Were we going to be shot?*

"It is him," I heard whispered in my ears.

"Who?" I mumbled, barely audible.

"Donnie."

"You think he was the killer?" Annabelle whispered nervously.

"We don't know if anybody is dead," I muttered.

The man walked over and took several items from the shelves and headed back upstairs. After the door closed, we let out a collective sigh of relief.

"How will we know if he leaves?" Linda asked, her voice shaky.

"We will just wait here for a while and listen," I told her.

We decided to lay down on the bed for a while and cover up. We were cold, scared, hungry and tired. Linda and Annabelle fell asleep, and I lay there and listened, though it didn't take long until I had fallen asleep as well.

When I woke up, I glanced around trying to remember where I was. I quickly pushed the cover down and got out of bed and stretched. Hesitantly, I climbed up the steps and listened for a while, and it was quiet.

CHAPTER NINE

After a few hours of silence in the house, I felt it was safe. I woke the girls and told them to be quiet, and that I was going to go upstairs as I felt it was safe. I then found some oil to put on the hinges, hoping to stop the creaky sound in case someone was still upstairs. I put the oil in one hand and the gun in the other and proceeded up the steps. I told them not come up for any reason as they begged me not to go.

"I will look around and come back for you," I said in a firm voice. When I reached the top step, I looked back and they had gotten under the bed. I oiled the hinges and pushed the door up. Once I was upstairs, I carefully put the door down and just stood and listened. It was eerily quiet; I could hear my heartbeat and my breaths sounded so loud in the silence. It was still dark outside so I had to use my flashlight as I made my way through the house.

As I walked across the creaky floors, my legs felt heavy as lead. I grasped the gun so tight; my hand was going numb. *I couldn't kill anyone if I had to,* I thought, *but maybe I could shoot him in the leg.* I searched the entire house thoroughly but saw no one. I sighed with relief and went back to the small door, knocked, and yelled for them to come up. They were so excited, they almost knocked me down as they reached the top.

"Can you guys fix the back door?" I asked, "I am in pain and I need to sit down.

They said "of course" and wrapped a blanket around me and helped me to the couch. As they were working on the back door; I was wondering about the mystery we had stumbled upon up Doc Polly Holler. *We are going to solve it no matter what,* I thought.

With the snow still falling outside and my still swollen ankle, we knew we would not be walking home any time soon. The girls fixed the door and made their way back to the living room and sat beside me.

"Do you think it would be safe to build a fire? "Annabelle asked.

"I don't know if it's safe enough, but we can't freeze," I said. "So, let's build a fire."

"I saw some wood just across the bridge," Linda mentioned.

"We can go get it," Annabelle suggested. "September, you stay here, rest your ankle."

They made sure I had enough blankets and a gun close by in case I needed to protect myself, then bundled up with flashlights and weapons in hand and made their way out the back door.

They returned not long after, racing through the door out of breath.

"What happened?" I asked.

"I dropped my flashlight when we were crossing the bridge and it fell into the creek," Linda said.

"And when we looked into the water, we saw a skull floating on the surface," Annabelle let out."

"We didn't get any wood."

"We'll have to grab some later. Anyone hungry?" I asked, trying not to let them see the fear that overwhelmed me.

"I will be back," I heard Linda say as she walked across the screechy floor toward the kitchen. Within a few minutes we were eating chicken noodle soup and each had a bottle of water. We were wondering if he would be coming back tonight or if he would wait till morning.

I was yawning so much, I had to go to sleep. I pushed my bowl under the couch, lay down and covered up, and soon fell asleep.

When I awoke, it was already daylight. I stood up and stretched and went to the kitchen and made us some tea. I thought I would fix us something to eat and sit at the table for the first time.

I opened a can of peaches, oranges, and apples, and arranged them on a plate, setting it on the table with a few forks for us. I then woke the girls and told them to come eat. As they walked toward the table, they were stretching.

"Wow September, this looks yummy," Linda said.

"Thank you," Annabelle added.

"I thought it was my turn, you guys have taken good care of me when my foot was really hurting," I said.

After our stomachs were full, we decided to go look for wood. I put the knife I had found in the building in the back of my pants in case we needed to cut some twigs.

"I'm not going back across the bridge," Linda said sternly.

"Don't worry were not," I said. We walked toward the door, but before we could get our guns, the door opens, we were now face to face with Donnie. He shoved us back inside pointing a gun at us. He pushed us into the chairs sitting at the table and tied our hands behind our backs. We were screaming, kicking and fighting.

"Don't go anywhere," he said, laughing as he walked up the stairs. After he was out of sight, I asked Linda and Annabelle if they could wiggle their hands loose.

We tried, but we couldn't. *We are doomed*, I thought, *unless we can get ourselves loose.* But we wore ourselves out trying.

"I've never been this scared since we got here. Oh, how I wish we were home," I mumbled. Then we heard Donnie coming back downstairs. He stood over us and began asking us questions.

"Who the hell are you, and what are you doing here?" he asked.

With quivering lips, I began to tell him who we were and that we were exploring. I explained that it had started pouring the rain and the door was ajar so we went inside to warm up.

"We thought the house was empty as the grass was long," I continued. "Then I twisted my ankle, and the heavy snow fell, so we couldn't walk the 4-miles back home. We were stranded."

"Did you see anything?" Donnie asked.

"No," Annabelle said sarcastically.

I was needing to pee really bad, so I asked if I could go to the bathroom.

"No," he said with an angry voice. So, I pleaded and pleaded. Finally, he yanked me up by the hair of my head and yelled, "Go, but don't try anything or I'll kill your friends."

I slowly walked up the steps and into the bathroom. As I began to pull my pants down, I discovered that I still had the knife. I shifted and felt the reassurance of the knife tucked away in the small of my back, between the elastic. I walked back down the steps and sat back down in the chair. He tied my hands back up and walked away. After about twenty minutes, I could hear snoring. I turned my head and on the couch the killer was sleeping and his gun lay on his stomach. My mouth moved but no sound came out.

"Knife," but my words were silent. Hoping they could read my lips, I continued, "Knife. behind my back, in my pants."

Linda nodded her head, and with her hand stretched out, she struggled to get it from me.

"Keep trying," I said, just moving my lips.

Finally, she lifted the knife and started cutting my hands free. After she freed me, she handed me the knife and I quickly cut them free.

"Run into the woods after we get outside," I whispered. They nodded their heads as if to say okay. We slowly tiptoed over to the door, hoping the floor wouldn't screech and wake Donnie up.

Once we reached the front door, we waited and watched for him to move, but he was still sleeping. I reached out my shaky hand and opened the door very slowly. We stepped outside and quietly closed the door behind us before rushing into the snow.

CHAPTER TEN

We ran as soon as our feet touched the ground until we found ourselves in the woods staring at a pile of rubbish and twigs that had been hiding under the melting snow.

"That looks like bones," I said as my fears worsened. I scraped my foot across the rubbish and saw more bones, mortified at the sight.

"We need to go and get a shovel and see what is covered up here." I exclaimed.

As I stood there, lost in my thoughts, staring at the bones, I heard what sounded like something or someone running behind me. Just as I turned around, Linda and Annabelle were standing behind me with the shovel. I reached out for the shovel, as Linda handed it to me, her hand trembled.

I began to dig just beneath the surface, and it felt like my heart stopped beating. I could see several more bones, and torn clothing. I dropped the shovel and ran, and the others were on my tail. Not knowing where we were going, we ended up at the car. As cold as I was, my shirt was sticking to my back from sweat. I was gasping for air and my heart was beating so fast that I thought it was going to jump out of my chest. I was getting dizzy, so, I jumped into the car and then fell unconscious. I came to when Linda slapped me in the face.

"We can go inside now, Linda said. "I think Donnie went out looking for us, but we must go now, so hurry," she cried. They helped my limp body out of the car and practically dragged me back to the house and helped me inside. They laid me behind the couch and covered me up, and then sat down beside me.

"She's in shock," I heard one of them whisper.

"She just needs to rest," the other one said.

Linda was giving me small drinks of water as they raised me to a sitting position.

"Are you feeling better, September?" Annabelle asked.

"Yes," I said with a soft whisper.

Suddenly, the door flung open. *If he finds us again, he will kill us this time,* I thought.

"He is a psychopath; he is responsible for a lot of deaths and he won't hesitate to kill us," I said and then warned them not to make a move or a sound. "We need to knock him out and tie him up, so he can spend the rest of his life in prison or maybe he'll get the death penalty," I surmised.

We heard Donnie march upstairs and Annabelle kneeled to look out the window.

"Get your ass back here now," I demanded.

As she pushed the curtain back to peek outside, she turned to us and said, "The snow is still melting."

Click!

Then a gunshot, and Annabelle hit the floor, blood oozing from her head.

"Oh my God, he killed her!" Linda screamed out.

"Shh! Quiet," I said, as I placed my index finger across my lips. Linda was clenching her fists and we were trying to hold back our loud breathing, thinking we would be next. The blood was running in our direction but we couldn't move as we watched her blood run underneath the soles of our shoes. The stairs creaked, pulling our attention away from the blood seeping into the floor. Donnie was coming towards us, a coy smile playing across his lips. He lowered the gun as he leaned closer and grabbed

Annabelle by the leg. He turned and dragged Annabelle's lifeless body behind him as he pulled her out the back door leaving a trail of blood.

"You stay here and I'll go look outside. I'll be right back, okay?" I said.

"No," she cried.

"I'll be right back, I promise," I said, trying to comfort her.

I rose to my feet and jogged across the screechy floor to the back door and glanced outside. Donnie was nearly out of sight, just beyond the tree line. With gun in hand, I ran across the bridge and hid behind some trees. As I looked through the trees, I could see him digging another hole in the same area we found the bones. Annabelle lay lifeless beside him, staining the snow a deep red. After a few moments of digging, he tossed the shovel aside and pulled Annabelle's body into the hole he'd created.

As I anticipated him turning back for the house to come after us, I was surprised when he jumped on a four-wheeler that was hidden in the woods and left the holler. I ran back to the house and didn't take time to shut the door as I ran to check on Linda. He knew we couldn't escape, so he wasn't concerned that we would get away and call the police. *He was going to kill us both*, I thought as I knelt to check on her.

"Did you find her?" she asked, tears running down her cheeks as she anxiously awaited my response.

"Yes," I said softly, "and he buried her." My heart was aching, and I figured that Linda's was too. We sat behind the couch and embraced each other as we sobbed from the loss of our dear friend. Feeling under the couch for my dirty cup that I had pushed under there earlier, I found a folder. Curious, I opened it and found the contents were notes from Dr. Timothy Sargent about a "Donnie Stump."

"Linda, what is Donnie's last name?" I asked.

"Stump," she replied.

I began to read.

Patient shows signs of Psychotic behavior, PTSD, and abuse. I asked him if I could hypnotize him, but he became very angry. He tried to stab me with a pencil, and threw everything off my desk. He lashed out and kicked and screamed at me. I called security and they came and restrained him so I could give him a shot to calm him down. He was admitted to a psych ward at a local hospital and is due to be released on August 1,1969.

This explains everything, I thought as I closed the folder. Then I felt around under the couch some more until my fingers landed on something else and I pulled it out. It was a small blue case like a cosmetic bag with a zipper. I looked inside and saw multiple bottles of medication that were full. Each had been prescribed to Donnie. It appeared as if he had quit or had never started taking them.

"When I hear the four-wheeler coming," I said, quickly turning to Linda, "I will hide behind the door with the poker and knock him out and tie him up."

"What?" Linda shrieked.

"Well, if you have a better idea, I'm listening," I snapped. The veins in my temple bulged out as I leaped from behind the couch and was suddenly knocked back onto the floor.

CHAPTER ELEVEN

"Linda," I squealed.

"It's a big dog September," Linda said, laughing hysterically. "I will go get him a Vienna sausage and he will get off you," she continued. The dog was heavy and began licking me so fiercely, I thought he was going to attack me, though he seemed friendly enough.

"Come here boy," Linda called, holding the sausage out in front of her. The dog leaped at her and snapped the sausage from her hand.

I'm okay, I thought, *just a little sore, few scratches and covered in slobbers.*

"It's a Bull Mastiff," Linda noted. "They are gentle and love children, and are protective and docile." It was a beautiful brindle color and wearing a red collar.

"Can you read the name on the dog tag?" I asked.

"It says, 'I belong to Bubba Snodgrass and my name is Kudda,'" Linda read.

"Well, if it lives here, there must be some dog food somewhere."

"I saw some buckets with lids on them down in the hidden room," Linda noted.

"Can you go check them out and I'll stay here?"

Linda seemed very excited to find a dog out here as she had a spring in her steps when she left to look for some dog food.

"Come here Kudda."

Kudda came toward me wagging his tail "Are you hungry boy?" I asked as I was patting his head. He began to lick me. "I'll get you some water boy, stay!" I grabbed a bowl from the kitchen and took it upstairs, carefully stepping around the space to the hidden room. I cleaned the bowl and filled it with fresh water and slowly made my way down the stairs just as Linda was coming up the steps below.

"Found some dog food," Linda said, with a big grin. We both loved dogs as we had one at our houses, Annabelle had too. We walked over to Kudda and sat down next to him as he ate. He was starving for sure; he quickly devoured all the food.

"More boy? Linda asked as she filled up the bowl, and he gobbled it up too, and then he took a drink of water.

"Feels better, huh Kudda?" I said. "Go lock the back door please, Linda, I don't want Kudda to get out, he will protect us." As I looked back down to pet him, he wasn't there. "Where is he?"

"He went upstairs," Linda said, pointing to the steps.

I stood and went for a bottle of water, wondering what Kudda was getting into upstairs.

"Bring me one," I heard.

"I was planning to," I said. I got us some water and hid back behind the couch. "I hope we don't get blamed for these murders because our fingerprints are on everything."

"I think his DNA will be found on the bodies, not ours, because we didn't get close to any of them. Maybe Annabelle's, because we were with her." Linda noted. "Besides, we didn't touch his gun," she continued.

"Hopefully," I added. *How are we going to explain Annabelle's death to her parents?* "Linda, do you think anyone is missing us?" I asked.

"Hell no!" she answered. "Not me anyway."

"I'm to blame for Annabelle dying because I shouldn't have brought you all out here," I said angrily. "Her parents are going to kill me."

"No September, we aren't little kids anymore, we came because we wanted to. I'll explain it to her parents and so will the police if we ever get out of this damn holler."

"Did you hear —"

But before I could finish, Linda answered, "Yes, it's him I bet."

"Remember our plan now," I reminded Linda.

I immediately grabbed the poker and told Linda to get ready to bring me the duct tape that we discussed earlier. I walked across the screechy floor and stood just behind the door so that when he opened it, I would jump out and hit him with the poker. I was consumed with anger as I stood in wait. As the sound of the four-wheeler neared the house, Kudda could hear it and he ran down the steps like he knew the sound. *Maybe Donnie had abused him,* I thought to myself. Kudda at the door with his tail down staring intensely, waiting for it to open.

I may not have to hit him after all, I thought. *Maybe Kudda would kill him.* I didn't want him dead, I wanted him to go to prison for the rest of his life. We could hear footsteps now on the porch. I raised my poker in anticipation, but when the door opened, Kudda attacked him immediately. He latched onto Donnie's leg and pulled him down, continuing to bite him. A pool of blood formed around his leg as the gashes got deeper with each bite.

"Linda come get the damn dog," I screamed. "Hurry." She pulled Kudda back and I hit

Donnie in the head with the fire poker, knocking him out.

"Come help me drag him over to that table," I demanded. "Let go of the damn dog and help me before he wakes up." We dragged his limp body over to the table and tied him up with an extension cord that I had cut off an old lamp earlier.

"You have the duct tape? hand it to me. Sorry Linda, I didn't mean to yell at you. I am just so mad at him for killing Annabelle," I said. Linda handed me the tape, then told me that she was sick and went behind the couch to lay down.

"Okay, I'll check on you when I tape him up," I said.

I taped his arms and legs and then put a piece across his mouth, careful not to cover his nose. I then wrapped him in duct tape, hoping he would not get loose before we could get the police. I watched his chest to make sure he was breathing, and thankfully he was. After I thought he was secure, I used a cloth to remove his gun from his side, careful not to leave my finger print, then went up the creaky steps and got a wet washcloth to put on Linda's forehead like my mom did for me when I was sick. She was pale and her face was hot to the touch.

"Linda, wake up," I pleaded, "please wake up." I put the washcloth on her forehead and soon she tried to sit up. She was mumbling something, but I couldn't understand her.

"It's okay now," I reassured her, "hold on and I'll get you some water, and I'll get you some applesauce also." I went to get water and applesauce and returned to her. As she took the food from me, she was shaking.

"I passed out," she said.

"I think you did," I said, hugging her and sobbing. "Can you stand up. now? I want to show you something." I could see she was still weak, but she was okay. We kept the weapons hid, but I made sure my knife was still tucked away in the small of my back. We walked over to where the killer lay tied up, and knelt beside him.

"Is he dead?" Linda asked.

"No, he's just knocked out, but maybe we can go home tomorrow on the four-wheeler," I told her. Donnie started moaning and trying to free himself, begging for water. Linda started kicking him and yelling at him.

"Hell no, you don't deserve water or to live for that matter." He began mumbling curse words at us and threatened to kill us.

"You should have killed us while you had the chance, you piece of crap!" Linda screamed in anger.

I didn't ever recall Linda being so angry, except for the time Annabelle and I stole her diary and read it and teased her about the crush she had on an older football player in high school. We had all been attending college this last year studying criminal science. We were supposed to graduate this year, but sadly Annabelle wouldn't be.

"September let's go look for Annabelle's body, okay?" Linda suggested.

"You don't want to see her, do you? Are you sure you can handle that?" I asked. Linda was already at the door waiting for me. With a sad heart, we walked out to the spot where we saw the bones before, and there lay Annabelle's topless body only partially buried.

"I bet that bastard raped her," Linda said tearfully.

"Probably so," I said angrily as the tears flowed down my cheeks. "I'll be right back Linda." I headed toward the house to get a blanket to cover up her body. As soon as I entered the house, my eyes shifted to the table where I had tied him and taped him up. I felt around my back for the knife, but it was gone. *I must have dropped it when we knelt beside him on the floor,* I thought. *Oh crap.*

I ran to get a second gun for Linda from behind the couch and collected a blanket then ran as fast as I could back to Linda, but when I returned to the grave, she wasn't there.

I was very worried that he may have gotten her too. I covered Annabelle's body and began screaming, "Linda! Where are you?" I continued calling out her name as I searched for her. I searched the car, and all around the area. I walked relentlessly through the woods and went across the narrow bridge, searching the water on both sides of the bridge. My heart was racing as I searched for a path I could take to check under the bridge.

CHAPTER TWELVE

finally found an overgrown path. Not worrying about anything except Linda's whereabouts, I headed down it, I didn't care what happened to me at this point; I figured he would kill us both eventually, and Linda could possibly be dead. I reached the bottom and began calling her name loud as I could. "Linda, please answer me, are you hiding somewhere?"

I stooped over to look under the bridge, and I could see the small skull lodged between two rocks. Before I could stand back up, Kudda was standing by my side barking profusely. "What is it boy? What do you see? Linda!" I screamed again. I knew he was seeing something I was not. I raised the gun and pointed it in the direction the dog was looking and barking. I then, out of the corner of my eye, saw weeds moving, but the wind wasn't blowing.

The dog ran, and I chased after him. As I was running, I saw a coat lying in the brush just ahead of me. I stopped and took a look and it was Linda's coat. *Oh damn, he is probably close by,* I thought, as I started running towards where I thought Kudda had gone. Almost immediately, I heard what sounded like a gunshot in the same direction I was going, but I continued on. *He must have another gun,* I thought.

Suddenly it was silent. "Please Lord, tell me he didn't kill the dog too," I cried. I couldn't stop crying, because now I was looking for Linda and the dog. I felt as though I was being followed; as soon as I heard a noise I would stop, then the noise would stop. I searched for nearly an hour before I found the dog Kudda lying in a small ditch with a gunshot to the head.

The blood was pooled just under his head, but I checked to make sure he was dead, and sadly he was.

I absolutely knew that Linda was dead somewhere, close to the dog's body, so I searched all around, but I didn't see her, and that gave me some hope that she might be hurt somewhere, but alive.

I continued my search and prayed for the Lord to show me where she was. But as usual, my mind was thinking the worse. I asked myself, *why was her coat laying back there?* Then I thought maybe there was a struggle and the coat may have gotten pulled off and that's why she got away. I could hardly breathe. By now I had searched for hours, but thankfully my ankle was better now. *If I find Linda, we're going home,* I said to myself, *if he doesn't kill me.*

He's out there, I know that. Suddenly I felt pain in the back of my head and was being dragged through the woods. I felt every rock and every stick that hit my back. It was cold and I was wet from the snow still on the ground.

I was wondering why he hadn't killed me yet, and I was in so much pain that I passed out. When I woke up, I was in the hidden room. It was very dark, and I had a horrible headache, but I got up and made my way up the steps and tried to push the door up, it wouldn't budge. I was trapped like a bear that had stepped in a trap. *Nobody would know I was down here, now that Linda is missing and probably dead.* I was talking to myself again, because it was lonely down there. I remembered a flashlight just under the bed where we had left it earlier, so I retrieved it. I lay on the bed and just cried and wondered how and when I would die. Then the door went up and a disgusting looking Donnie was approaching me.

I searched for the gun, but he must have taken it when he hit me in the head. I now knew what he was going to do to me, and that's why he didn't kill me yet. He brought me some water and food. *If he was planning on killing me, he wouldn't have brought me anything,* I thought. He loomed closer to me with the food, and I knocked it onto the floor.

His grubby hands were now pulling my wet pants down as I fought him, but it didn't help. I said no, I kicked and screamed, and begged even. He just laughed at me. I was crying so hard, but it didn't matter to him. He was very wicked and my skin crawled at his touch. He set his gun on the shelf where the food was, and out of my reach. I could only imagine what Linda was going through, if she was still alive.

"Man, are you a virgin?" he asked as he forced himself inside me. I wanted to die I felt so dirty. "You liked it and you know it," he said. After he finished, he said he'd be back to give me more. I waited for him to leave, then I got up and wiped myself with the corner of the sheet. Thankful we didn't take all the food upstairs; I got myself a can of pork n beans and popped the lid and drank them because I needed to keep up my strength, but I didn't want him to know. I saved the can in case I could make a weapon out of it, so I hid it under the bed.

I lay back down after I peed in a bucket that was sitting in the corner, and cried myself to sleep while hoping Linda was still alive and would find me. When I woke up, I began to try and figure out how to sharpen the can. I searched the whole room and couldn't find anything sharp, so I began rubbing the can on the cinder block wall until my arms were sore. I was afraid he would see the shavings on the floor, so I raked them under the bed with my hand.

Suddenly dread came upon me when I heard a scraping noise upstairs; he was moving something off the door and coming down here again. As he was coming downstairs, I pretended to be asleep, hoping he would leave me alone, but instead, he got on top of me after pulling my pants down. I was in shock and could only lay still hoping it would end soon.

He was inside me and I hated it. I didn't see food this time, but he had water. His breath reeked of alcohol as he kissed me. It was hard to lay still because I wanted to vomit. I continued to pray for help, but none came. After he finished, I fought him, knowing I couldn't win.

He punched me in the face, and I could taste the bitter blood as it dribbled past my lips and onto my shirt.

"Bitch!" he screamed. "You stupid bitch."

The next time he comes down here, I will kick him in the nuts, I thought to myself. Finally, he left again, and I heard him push something over the door. As soon as he left, I wiped myself again and grabbed a bottle of water and washed my mouth out over and over util the bottle was empty. I opened another bottle and took a drink and hid the water under the bed, so he would think I was out and bring me more. I got the can and began to try to sharpen it on the cinder block wall again.

It was quiet down there, so I began a cheer I had learned when I was a cheerleader: *Bobo See Rotten Trotten.* I repeated it through the day to keep myself occupied as the hours went on. I had to stay sane if I wanted to escape this dreadful place that had become my prison, my personal hell.

CHAPTER THIRTEEN

I had already been down here a week and I was not going to take it anymore. I was working on my escape plan every day. I looked for paper and pencil so I could keep track of the days, but there wasn't any. So, I had to brainstorm. I crawled under the bed up against the wall, and with my finger I wrote day 1, day 2 and so on. I carefully scooted myself out without erasing what I had written. *The next time he comes to rape me, I'm going to fight like hell.* I didn't care if he killed me or not, because I was dead already inside and it was only a matter of time before he would kill me anyway.

On the eighth day, he thought I would be weak because I refused to eat the food, he brought me, but I wasn't as I'd been eating food left down there. I had to fight for my life if I wanted to find Linda and go home. *This is the day I will escape this dreadful room and this horrible man.* As he came down the steps, I again acted like I was asleep, but I had my now sharp can under my pillow and I was going to cut his throat, hopefully just enough for me to get away.

He was the evilest person I had ever seen or heard of in my life. It was terrifying that he may kill me, but I was going to fight him even if he did. As he wobbled towards me, I saw the gun, but as usual he laid it on the shelf. My body clenched as he pulled down my pants again, and my skin crawled as he put himself inside me. As he was enjoying the moment, I put my hand under the pillow and grabbed the can, and in one swift movement, whipped it out and swiped it across his neck. He fell off of me and hit the floor, clenching his throat.

I grabbed everything that I thought he could use to escape, including his gun and the knife, and ran as fast as I could and bound up the steps, then closed the door and slid the desk over it.

I ran outside to get some fresh air and the brightness outside blinded me after only having the light of a flashlight for a week. After I got some fresh air, I went back in and walked across the screechy floor and put my ear against the door and listened for any sound, but it was quiet.

With him stuck in the hidden room, I had to get the stench of him off of me, so I ran upstairs and ran some water in the tub. The water was cold, but I didn't care. I felt so dirty I scrubbed till my skin hurt. When I finished, I went back downstairs and looked for some clothes. I remembered the clothes we had found in the trunk; I walked over to the pile and found a pair of sweats and a shirt and put them on.

It was still daylight out, so I decided to look for Linda. *I would scream out to her that Donnie was dead and maybe she would come out of hiding if she was in fact alive,* I thought. I walked aimlessly through the woods, yelling, "He's dead Linda, I locked him down in the hidden room. Come out if you're hiding or yell if you are hurt. Linda!" I continued to yell at the top of my lungs. I suddenly stopped dead in my tracks because I thought I heard a noise. Birds were singing from the treetops and the wind was blowing fiercely now, the trees were swaying back and forth. I listened and I thought I heard a faint cry over in the area of the old house. I spun around immediately and ran fast as I could, praying it was Linda. I ran faster.

I tripped and fell a couple times, but I just got up and continued running towards the house. "Keep making a noisenda so I can find you!" I yelled.

Finally, I heard a resounding voice cry out, "I'm under the porch!" Suddenly I was standing in front of the same house I was wanting to flee from, but I couldn't go without Linda. I stood in front of the porch when suddenly something touched my leg. A hand was outstretched and was grabbing for my ankle. I bent over and saw Linda under the porch, so I ducked under.

"Oh my God Linda," I screamed with excitement. "Have you been here the whole time? Do you think you could make it into the house if I help you?"

She moaned a faint, "I think so." I could tell he beat the hell out of her. I carefully helped her out from under the porch and helped her into the house, assisted her in lying down on the couch, then went to get her water and a quilt. When I returned, I checked her out and she had several broken ribs, lots of bruises, some scrapes, a black eye and a bleeding lip.

"You are going to be okay now," I assured her, "try get some sleep and we will talk when you wake up, I promise, I'll be right here." It was bothering me about what I would say to her if she asked me about Kudda. I glanced at her and she was sound asleep. I decided to build a fire to warm her up. The warmth of the fire felt so good as the flicker of the flames brought me some relaxation that I desperately needed. I walked quietly, so not to wake Linda, to the little door and placed my ear down against it. All I could hear was moaning. I was thankful he was alive so he could die in prison. It dawned on me that he may be able to lift the door up with just the desk on it, so I used the last of the nails we had and nailed it down to make sure. I decided that I would sleep on the floor next to Linda, so I grabbed myself a blanket and lay down. Before long I was asleep.

When I woke up, Linda was already up and, in the kitchen, fixing food. As she walked toward me with the food, I could tell she was in a lot of pain. As we were sitting on the couch eating, we could hear Donnie pounding fiercely on the small door that led down to the hidden room. Linda began to scream as she thought he would get out and finish us off.

"No Linda, he's not getting out, I promise. I'm going to wrap your ribs, so relax and I'll be right back. Okay?" I went upstairs and took a sheet off one of the twin beds and wrapped it tightly around her ribs. She screamed, but I told her it would help her pain.

CHAPTER FOURTEEN

"Okay, are you ready to tell me what happened to you?" I asked.

She began, "I was okay one minute and then I felt a horrible pain in the back of my head the next minute. I was knocked unconscious. When I woke, I found myself in the trunk of the car. I wasn't sure how long I had been in there, but he periodically yanked me out of the trunk and took me into the woods and raped me, and beat the hell out of me every time I fought back. The last time he raped me, I kicked him in the balls, and when he fell to the ground clutching himself, I picked up a piece of wood and hit him in the head.

"I walked out the holler until I couldn't see the house anymore. It took me quite a while to make it to the mouth of the holler because of my injuries. Then I saw a house and knocked on the door, a little old lady answered, but she seemed to be scared of me. I told her what was going on up Doc Polly Holler and asked her to go get the police. She told me that the next time she goes to town, she would tell the police. She gave me a bottle of water then I headed back here to tell you. I was worn out and in a lot of pain by the time I returned. As I approached the porch, I saw him out of the corner of my eye, but I was too tired and sore to run, so I dashed under the porch.

"I searched around the car, but it was stupid of me not check the trunk," sorry Linda, I told her.

"So, do you think she will get the police to come out here?" I asked, feeling somewhat relieved, but at the same time, I wept for her.

"I don't know," she said, "Now your turn, September."

"Okay. It was same as you pretty much," I began.

"I was hit in the back of the head and knocked unconscious while I was searching for you, and when I woke up, I was locked in the hidden room. He went down there every day and raped me for seven days. I counted the days by writing it in the dirt under the bed.

I had been sharpening a can by rubbing it against the cinder block wall, and kept it under my pillow. When he came downstairs today, I pretended to be asleep. As he was forcing himself inside me, I grabbed the can and swiped it across his neck. He hit the floor and I grabbed everything I thought he could use to escape, careful not to leave finger prints on the gun or knife, and ran like a bat out of hell. I nailed the door shut with him down there, and here we are safe and sound... I hope."

"Do you think we should gather all the evidence we found, in case he has an accomplice, and put it in a safe place?" I asked.

"Probably a good idea," Linda replied. "Did you get the gun he'd been using?" She stood from the couch slowly.

"I sure did," I said. "So, if you feel like it, let's get this done in case the police show up. We can gather everything and lock it safely in the trunk of the car." We emptied the box that was under the table and put the notebook in there and his two guns, the bottles of medication and the folder from Donnie's psychiatrist, and the knife.

Neither one of us wanted to go get the shovel, but we wanted to make sure we had all the evidence.

We left the house with the box and walked toward the grave site, with tears running down our cheeks and very hesitantly. I couldn't bear to see Annabelle's body again, although I had covered it up, but we proceeded anyway because we were wanting to help solve this crime. After we reached the grave site, I grabbed the shovel and turned away.

Both of us were heavy hearted, and our eyes were filled with tears. We arrived at the car and popped the trunk, then put all we had in the trunk for the police.

"Let's make sure we have everything," I said. I got the keys and unlocked the car door and grabbed the hair brush from the dash of the car.

Linda got the book bag and gathered the contents from the seat and the floorboard, I got the shirt and the clothes from the floorboard in the front.

"That's it," Linda said, so we put the evidence in the trunk and closed it, and locked all the doors. Feeling so much sorrow in our hearts for Annabelle, we slowly, even dragging our feet at times, walked back to the house. As soon as I pushed the door open, I ran immediately over to the small door and placed my ear on it and listened. All I could hear was him groaning.

"If the police don't come soon, we'll have to give him water," I explained.

"Oh, hell no!" Linda screamed. "I want to go home now," she cried.

"Me too," I responded, "but no matter what he did, we can't kill him; we are not killers. Maybe the police will show up soon."

Linda and I were just chilling on the couch and sipping tea, and talking about riding the 4-wheeler home, when the loud sound of sirens approached. We jumped up and ran outside and cops were everywhere. It was so exciting to see and we could hardly control our emotions. Choppers were hovering around, ambulances, firetrucks, coroner vans, CSI vans. It was a wonderful sight. *We did it,* I thought, *I just wish Annabelle could see.*

"We are going to be alright now, Linda," I said with enthusiasm and excitement. A detective walked over to us and cordially asked if we were okay, and we of course said yes.

"My name is Detective Hollister," he said, and informed us that a lady had called him about the situation out here. "Can you give me your statement? "he continued.

"Yes, of course," I replied. He then took me to the police car and I told him everything, then it was Linda's turn, and she told him everything I assumed. I informed the detective that I had locked Donnie in the hidden room and he may need medical attention.

The detective told me to stay put, so I stood on the porch and waited as he walked to the ambulance and returned with two paramedics and a gurney.

"Okay, now show me where he's at," one of the officers requested.

"This way sir," I said as I led them to the small door hidden under the rug at the bottom of the steps. I pointed to the desk and said, "Under there, sir." He asked me to stay put as he raised the door, with his gun drawn, he proceeded down the steps.

"This is Agent McCall and I'm with the FBI, coming down now," he informed Donnie. I could see him examining Donnie and then he yelled to the other Detective to go get the paramedics and bring down the gurney. I could smell feces and urine escaping from the room. The Detective told me to go wait on the porch, so I did. Linda was standing on the porch already.

"Did you tell him where the bodies were?" I asked.

"Of course, I told him everything from the beginning," Linda added.

The CSI was taping off the whole area, for it was a crime scene. They were taking lots of photographs from all angles. They looked for casings from firearms, slugs that may have missed the victims, footprints, fingerprints, and places where the crimes may have occurred. Several coroners headed toward the grave site carrying body bags. They were gone a long time because they had to collect body fluids from under the remains, fluids that may have leaked out or have been deposited from the person who committed the crime. They had to log evidence and I always heard they treated bodies with the utmost respect.

It seemed to take hours getting Donnie upstairs, but finally they managed. As the gurney went past us, we were disgusted by him. We watched as they loaded the worthless piece of shit into the ambulance and drove away.

Still standing on the porch, we saw the coroners come out of the woods with several body bags, and one came from the back of the house carrying what looked to be the skull from the creek. They placed them in the van and drove away. It was nearly dark, so they installed lots of lighting outside so they could continue their investigation.

I overheard a conversation between two officers as they said this was one of the largest crime scenes and the most horrific, they had ever seen. The expressions on their faces revealed much sadness.

CHAPTER FIFTEEN

Detective Hollister and Agent McCall wanted us to go home, but we refused to leave.

"We need to see this through because we were his victims too," I explained.

"Okay but you will have to avoid all the crime scenes," he noted.

"Okay," I agreed, and continued to remind him that they wouldn't have Donnie if it wasn't for us.

"We will need both of your fingerprints and you may be called to testify when this goes to trial," he continued.

"Our fingerprints will be on everything," I explained, "because we gathered up all the evidence you got out of the trunk of the car."

"You two can stay on the couch or on the front porch," he informed us. "We have been searching for Donnie Stump and the fourteen-year-old Misty Higgins for quite some time," he added. The door opened and 8- CSI investigators walked in; 3 went down in the hidden room, 3 went upstairs, and 2 stayed down here. They worked through the night dusting for fingerprints, taking photos, sketching things, and documenting everything. Detective Hollister gave Linda and I a hamburger, fries, and a coke. It was delicious because we had been surviving on canned goods, water, cold coffee and cold tea for nearly two weeks.

The CSI detectives were methodical in their investigation and collecting evidence. They had gathered lots of evidence including Annabelle's blood that was thick and drying on the floor.

Agent McCall was questioning us about the stuffed animal with blood on it that was under the tractor. I also told him about the birthday card that said "Happy 1st Birthday Lilly! Love always, Dad" but all that was burned up now. He said they are searching for remains in the ashes, hoping to find some chard bones, if a baby had been buried there.

The female CSI investigators all had short hair and were not wearing makeup, so I asked why. He informed me that it was to keep from contaminating the crime scenes.

"I am in my last year of college and I want to be a CSI," I told him.

"Great," he replied. "What about you Linda?"

"I'm in my last year also and I also want to be a CSI," she explained.

"Wow ladies you are going to be great at your jobs. Look what you have uncovered in this investigation," he said in a complimentary voice. "Did you girls know there was a reward from Annabelle's parents and the police?" he asked.

"No," we both answered at the same time.

"How much?" Linda asked with enthusiasm.

"$40,000 for Donnie's apprehension, and $10,000 for the whereabouts of Annabelle, and $20,000 for the whereabouts of Misty. Plus, after the conviction of Donnie, you all can write a book about your experience out here, and maybe they will want to make a movie based on your book," he told us.

"Oh my God!" we screamed as we jumped up and embraced each other.

"Okay ladies, calm down now," Agent McCall urged us, "you have to go home tomorrow, but we will stay in touch I promise. So maybe you should get some sleep now."

We were very tired so we fell asleep on the couch pretty quick, when we woke up it was daylight and the detectives were still at it, sketching and measuring things.

Detective Hollister is a handsome man, but a little too old for me, I thought. Agent McCall was a heavy-set man and was very nice to us. Detective Hollister handed us a sausage biscuit and an orange juice and told us that our parents were informed and they knew we were safe.

We went to the front porch to eat our breakfast. As we ate, we thought about having to leave without Annabelle, returning to school without her, Christmas, birthdays, her funeral and court, and how we survived, but Annabelle didn't. The detective told us we would be going home shortly. When it was time to leave, we followed the detective to the police car and got in.

We stared back at the old house as the car was leaving Doc Polly Holler. We gave him our addresses and he dropped Linda off first and then me. My parents burst into tears of joy when they met me at the door. At the supper table, they wanted to know everything. It took several hours but I explained everything.

"I'll make you an appointment with a therapist in the morning, it will help you," Mom insisted. "You girls are already heroes," she continued as she stood to clear the table, "your faces are all over the television. I'm so sorry to hear about Annabelle, September. I know the three of you were best friends, and it's not your fault."

"Need help Mom?" I asked.

"No sweety, you get some rest, I'm fine," she answered. "I'm so glad you're safe September."

"Glad to be home Mom," I said. I went upstairs to my room, and it was definitely good to be back in my own room. I flopped across my bed and looked through some photos of the three of us and the school yearbook. I cried as I thumbed through the pages because Annabelle was posing silly in a lot of them, there were vacation photos, birthday photos, and Christmas photos. The yearbook had our cheerleader photos and more. I put everything under the bed and flipped the light out and cried myself to sleep, exhausted from the long day.

I woke up screaming from a nightmare. Mom heard me and came running in and sat with me until I fell back to sleep.

When mooring came, I ran down the steps and sat down at the table for breakfast. I then asked Mom if she would take me to Linda's and she reminded me I had an appointment with the therapist, but she would take me afterwards.

I was not looking forward to going and talking about my rape with a stranger. After arriving, I went and checked in. "September," they called, I followed them to a room down the hall and sat and waited for the doctor, chewing on my nails and twirling my hair as I waited. The door finally opened and a woman stretched out her hand and introduced herself as Dr. Watson.

"Nice to meet you," I said. She took down a lot of information and then I began telling her the nightmare of what had happened at the house up Doc Polly Holler. I cried through it all. She prescribed me an antidepressant and made me a follow-up appointment for the following week.

I met up with Mom and she took me to Linda's house. As we pulled into the driveway, I saw Annabelle's mom Jennifer's car. I was hesitant about going in, but Linda met me at the door and told me that Jennifer didn't blame either one of us for Annabelle's death. As I stepped inside, I was met with Jennifer, her arms stretched out ready to embrace me. We sobbed together as she held me.

"Linda, she went with you all because she loved being around you. And besides, you couldn't have known about the hell that you all would have to endure."

Later as we were sitting on the couch, they discussed the funeral, although her body wouldn't be released for at least a week. They were making the arrangements today, but Linda and I went to her room and threw ourselves on her bed.

"Do you have nightmares?" I asked.

"Yes, I do, and they are so real," Linda answered.

"Mom took me to see a therapist and I have another appointment next week. Maybe you should go see one," I added. I stayed for a few hours and then went home.

After a long week, it was time for Annabelle's funeral. I dreaded it, but I had to go out of respect.

The day of the funeral, we stood outside the funeral home and everyone's heads were down, maybe out of respect or maybe they were afraid to look at what was next.

The casket was purple as it was Annabelle's favorite color. The casket was pulled from the hurst and carried by 6 of our friends all dressed in black suits. The silence dwelled as they entered the church, carrying her casket to the front, and gently set it down on a dark colored catafalque.

The flowers were arranged beautifully, and the lid was raised and the casket had a silky cushioned lining. Annabelle was as beautiful as she was in life, and looked so peaceful. Jennifer was distraught as she held my hand and leaned on me. I was holding myself together until they played the video of her in life having so much fun. Linda and I fell apart. I know it's silly, but I was hoping she would get up and go home, but I realized she was gone.

I said my final goodbye as the funeral ended and they closed the lid. The music played softly as the pallbearers carried her back to the hurst. There wasn't a dry eye anywhere as the cars lined up behind the hurst.

The funeral procession began to take Annabelle to her final resting place. When we arrived at the cemetery and before they put the casket in the ground, Linda and I placed a lily on her casket — her favorite flower.

"Mom, can we leave now?" I asked.

"Of course honey," she replied. It seemed like a long trip back home because our hearts were filled with so much sadness. Upon entering the house, the phone was ringing.

"Hello?" I answered.

The voice on the other end said, "Hello, this is Detective Hollister, may I speak to September?"

"This is she," I responded.

"Can I drop by your house around four o'clock? I'd like to bring you something."

"Sure," I agreed, then I said bye, and hung up the phone. I was hoping he was bringing us the reward money. I told mom that he was coming and she said she would make coffee and some finger food to offer him.

"Thanks Mom, that sounds great," I said as I went to call Linda to tell her that the Detective was coming, possibly with the reward money. She was so excited that she just said, "Okay bye, I'll see you in a bit," and hung up the phone. When Linda arrived, we went up to my room. As soon as we lay across the bed, there was a knock at the front door.

"I'll get it," my mom yelled up to us. We ran down the steps and standing just outside was Detective Hollister. "Come in please, I'm Rebecca, September's mom. Have a seat on the couch and I'll get you a cup of coffee."

He sat down beside us and reached in his pocket and pulled out two envelopes, handing me one and Linda the other. We were beside ourselves with excitement as we opened the envelopes and pulled out what we hoped would be our checks. With a loud voice I screamed,

"My check is for $35,000; how much is yours Linda?" I asked.

"Same as yours," she said, smiling from ear to ear.

"Are they finished with the investigation at the house up Doc Polly Holler?" I asked.

"Yes," Detective Hollister said. "Donnie Stump was charged with seven counts of 1st degree murder, 4 counts of rape, arson and kidnapping.

"No bond was set in his case." Linda and I were overcome with joy that Annabelle's murder wasn't in vain, as it helped to solve 6 other murders.

"He'll most likely get the death penalty, so he can never hurt anyone again. We recovered the remains of six other victims and we're now in the identification process," he continued. "I have to go, that's all I can share with you. I'll be in touch," he said and left.

That year, Linda and I graduated college and got great jobs as CSI investigators. I went to many crime scenes, but one stood out to me involving a 6-year-old little girl named Lexi Newsome. Lexi was a beautiful little girl with a contagious smile. Her long blonde hair was in pigtails the day she went missing and she was the only child of the Newsome's. She had to walk out a long driveway lined with trees to get to her house after she was dropped off by the school bus. On April 5, 1978, she never made it home after school. Cecil Hopkins kidnapped her and held her in a cellar.

During the three years he held her there, he raped and tortured her. Her tiny body had washed up after flood water had receded. The coroners determined that the cause of death was asphyxia. Cecil was arrested and charged with first degree murder, torture, and kidnapping.

After this case was closed, I moved to Florida, and Linda stayed near her family in Madison, WV. We both had wonderful husbands and two kids each.

CHAPTER SIXTEEN

Linda and her family were on their way to visit me for Christmas in 1989, when my phone rang. It was Linda's mother.

"Her plane crashed about 3000 feet past the runway and there were no survivors." The voice on the other end of the line was crying uncontrollably.

"What?" No survivors? I cried, inconsolable as I screamed into the phone.

"They were all on the plane," she said.

I got off the phone and sat and cried, because I would have to be part of the forensic team to go to the wreckage site. I wasn't sure if I could, but it was my job. I was distraught because she was the second one to die out of my 2 best friends. I dreaded it. When I arrived at the site, bodies and parts of the plane was scattered about. Twisted metal was hiding most of the bodies. Coroners were already there and overseeing the collection of physical, scientific, and pathological evidence, and the scene was already taped off.

I began to photograph the scene, did many sketches and measurements before anything was collected and packaged.

I was doing my job professionally, but I was also in search of Linda and her family. The NTSB, FAA, FBI and state and local authorities were all on the scene. It took two days to find Linda. When I found her body, she was strapped in her seat and looked as if she was asleep, her limbs twisted and mangled, burned but recognizable. I literally had to throw up, not because I haven't seen horrific scenes, but because I loved her. I never found her family though. I continued my job but photographing my best friend's mangled body was killing me inside, though it didn't prevent me from doing my job professionally.

As I was bent over getting a closeup photo of Linda, someone touched my shoulder. As I turned around, I was surprised to see an FBI agent whom I recognized as Hannah. Hannah, Linda, Annabelle and I had history. Hannah had stolen my boyfriend Jeff in high school. Because of her lies. Hannah and I fought often and weren't friends.

We chatted a bit, then she handed me a piece of paper with her phone number and said, "Call me some time," then walked away. Trying not to get angry, I continued my job.

Just as I was finishing up, I saw off in the distance a coroner that looked familiar to me. I began to walk closer, and sure enough, it was my high school sweetheart Jeff.

"Oh my God, Jeff? it's me, September," I said.

"What have you been into September?" Jeff asked.

"I'm a CSI investigator now, and my friend Linda and her family were on this plane," I told him.

"Oh, that's horrible. I remember Linda. How is Annabelle?" he asked.

"She was murdered back in '69, didn't you hear? I asked. Then his phone rang and tore his attention away. It was on speaker so I could hear his conversation, and realized he was talking to his wife Hannah. I waved bye to him and walked away. I knew I wasn't going to call Hannah, so I threw away her phone number.

We were at the crash site for at least two weeks. The black boxes were recovered and analyzed and it was determined that the plane had engine failure. Linda was thirty-eight years old when she died and Annabelle was murdered at age twenty.

This crime scene was by far the worst ever, and I was hoping I would never have to go to another plane crash site. After all the remains were identified and returned to loved ones, Linda, like the others had a closed casket funeral, because their bodies were, in most cases, burned badly. After Linda and her family were buried, I was sitting at home and was thinking about what Detective Hollister had told us about writing a book about our ordeal up Doc Polly Holler.

So, I started writing our story, but hated to do it without my two best friends.

It was November 13, 1969. The three of us were taking a walk and stumbled upon an old abandoned house up Doc Polly Holler in Madison, West Virginia. It was a cold day, but we didn't mind because we were twenty years old without a care in the world.

Then I stopped for a while and thought about the whole ordeal we had gone through. How we were repeatedly raped, how close we came to dying, and witnessing Annabelle's murder and the fear that caused us nightmares. My mind drifted to Donnie and what was happening in his case, but realized I had moved and maybe Detective Hollister couldn't find me now. I wondered if he heard about Linda. I was having a hard time concentrating on the book I was writing as my mind was running away with me. *Could Donnie be dead? Maybe he is on death row, or maybe he escaped and is coming to finish the job?*

My husband, Derick, and kids Olive and Buster were in West Virginia visiting family for a week and I took a week off from my job to work on my book.

I kept noticing a car going by my house several times a day, but could I just be paranoid? After I cleared my head a little, I started writing again, but was interrupted by a car parked in front of my house revving the engine. I walked over to the window and peeked out, but I couldn't see who was inside because the windows were tinted.

I was now being stalked, I told myself. After I heard the car speed away, I took a shower and went to bed. The next morning after breakfast, I got dressed and went to a different grocery store. When I drove into the parking lot in front of the store, I saw a car identical to the one that sat in front of my house. One of the windows was down so I could see inside, but the car was empty.

Oh my God! They could be in the store! I told myself, my heart racing with every step I took toward the door. I was trembling as I stepped inside, hoping no one would recognize me as the girl from the house up Doc Polly Holler, but my story was a national news story, so I tried not to be noticed. I grabbed a cart and was making sure that I was aware of my surroundings the whole time, I walked quickly through the aisles. After getting my groceries, I hurried to the checkout.

"September is that you?" someone asked.

"Yes, it's me," I answered. It was a gray-haired older woman at the register.

"I was Donnie's girlfriend when he attacked you and your friends," the woman said as she continued ringing up my items. "We lived in Charleston, West Virginia for a while until he hurt me, then I ran him off."

"Well, I have to run," I said, cutting the conversation short as I finished paying for my groceries.

I loaded my cart and practically ran to my car. I popped the trunk and put my groceries inside and jumped in the car. As I started my engine, I looked and the car was still there, and the window was up. I pulled out slowly to see if the person would follow me, and sure enough they did. I took a lot of different turns on my way home to make sure they were really following me, and not just my imagination, the car was getting closer, so I sped up and hurried home. When I parked in my driveway, I hopped out and left the groceries in the trunk.

My hands trembled as I tried to insert the key into the keyhole. After I unlocked the door, I ran inside and slammed the door behind me and immediately locked all the locks. The car had pulled onto the driveway right beside mine. I stood by the window waiting for the car to leave so I could get my groceries. It was dark when the car finally left, so I turned the lights on outside so I could see to get my groceries.

I was panicked as I gathered my groceries and ran back into the house. I put everything away and went to the gun cabinet and got a shotgun and loaded it.

I didn't want to call and worry my family, so I wrote until it was time to go to bed. My eyes were tired from all the writing, so I took my gun to the bedroom with me and laid it down beside me on the bed. During the night I was awakened by loud cracks of thunder that sounded like two bowling balls clanging together, and the lightning was trying to enter the widow through the opening in the curtains.

I couldn't sleep. I got up and started working on my book again and placed the gun next to me. The rain was pounding loudly on my metal roof, and it was hard to hear anything else. My stomach was growling, so I went to the kitchen to make popcorn. As I was waiting for my popcorn to pop, I thought I saw a shadowy figure outside the window in the darkness of night. I could see the dark figure every time lightning would strike and light up the sky.

However, I convinced myself that no one would be stupid enough to be out in this storm. But after seeing that car in front of my house and now being stalked by someone, I wasn't going to take any chances, so I carried the gun everywhere I went.

To reassure myself that I hadn't seen anyone or anything, I went through the entire house and looked out every window. After I finished doing that, I thought I heard a noise in front of the house, so I walked nervously to the living room and someone was jiggling my doorknob. Thinking someone may kick the door open, I sat in my recliner with the shotgun, pointing it straight at the door just in case they did.

I had a deadbolt installed because of what happened up Doc Polly Holler. Since I hadn't heard from Detective Hollister, it was a real possibility that Donnie Stump had escaped and he was here to kill me because I had gotten away. After all, he had murdered 6 people, not counting Annabelle and evaded the police for quite some time. If it weren't for Linda, Annabelle, and myself, it's hard to tell how long he would have been at large and maybe killed more people. He was a psychopath and definitely smart enough to escape police custody.

Donnie was twenty-three-years old when he got arrested and he would be fifty-two now, so I probably wouldn't recognize him. I would always recognize his voice though, no matter how old he was. His voice was toneless but strident at times.

I distinctly remembered a tattoo on his right forearm; a snake wrapped around a dagger. As I thought more about what he may look like, I remembered the time I cut his neck with a steel can. *That should have left an ugly scar,* I thought.

CHAPTER SEVENTEEN

Finally, the doorknob wasn't jiggling anymore, thankfully, so they must have given up and left. I went back to bed and fell asleep and slept pretty well. The next morning at about 9 o'clock, I took a shower and fixed breakfast. After breakfast, I started writing again. I was up to the part where we found the skeletal remains in the woods. There were only 4 more days until my family was to come back and I had to return to work, so I wanted to write as much as I could. I always listened to the news hoping to hear something about Donnie, but I reminded myself that a lot of time had passed, so it probably wouldn't be on the news anymore.

I began to wonder that if he did escape, maybe he would be on America's Most Wanted, so I got on my computer and began to search. I went to their website and searched Donnie Stump, then they wanted to know the state where he was from, so I typed in West Virginia. *Holy shit!* A name popped up with a photo. The person in the photo was fifty-two years old, charged with 7 counts of murder, rape, and kidnapping, last seen wearing a dark blue suit with a light blue shirt and yellow tie, after escaping from the courthouse on August 17, 1974 in a white Monte Carlo with a woman driving it.

It went on to say that he was very dangerous and not to approach him, but to call the hotline number. The man in the image I was staring at was morbidly obese, had a long scraggly beard.

She was described as being petite and had short brown hair, and approximately forty-four years old, last known sighting of the couple was at a nightclub in Charleston, West Virginia on June 7, 1978. It was now September 27, 1990.

It was day 3 of me being harassed and stalked. The car I saw was not a white Monte Carlo, but a yellow older model Ford Mustang. I began to make plans to see my stalker's face. I came up with several ideas, but I ended up calling my neighbor behind my house.

"Hello," the voice on the phone answered.

"Hello Rachel, this is September, can I borrow your car?" I asked.

"Yes, of course you can," she replied.

"Okay I'll come over and get the keys shortly, if it's okay with you, then I'll come get the car later."

"That's fine."

"Okay see you then. Bye!" After about thirty minutes, I went out my back door and across the street to Rachel's house and got the keys.

I was going to follow the car to see if it was Donnie Stump. Once back inside my house, I waited anxiously for the yellow mustang to return, hoping it would return before dark so I could see his face. Then the sound of a car horn blasting announced their arrival. I went over to the window and peeped outside and sure enough it was the yellow mustang that had parked in my driveway beside my car.

I disguised myself by wearing a cap with my hair pinned up and went out the back door, hoping not to be seen by the driver of the mustang. I then went to get my neighbors car and drove around the block until he decided to leave my house. Looking out of the side mirror, I saw him back out of my driveway.

I got behind him trying to keep a safe distance so he wouldn't know he was being followed. I followed him for about ten miles when he pulled into a parking lot of an apartment complex. I parked 2 car lengths from him and waited for him to get out. I had my eyes fixed on him when he finally got out of the car, walked past the car that I had I borrowed, and went in the apartment at the end of the complex: apartment number 3.

My heart was racing as my mind went back to the horror I had experienced up Doc Polly Holler. *Oh my God it was him,* I said to myself, *he is here to kill me.* I was now panicking, just hoping to get home safe. I put the car in reverse and sped home, hoping I would get pulled over by the police. *How in the hell did he find me?* I wondered. After getting home, I returned the car to my neighbor and gave her the keys.

"Are you okay?" Rachel asked, "You look like you've seen a ghost." She laughed.

"I'm good thank you, but I have to go now," I said. I rushed back to my house overwhelmed with fear, and quickly ran inside and locked all the locks. I then picked the phone up and called the number for the hot line posted on Americas Most Wanted website and reported that I had seen Donnie Stump. I left all the information on their voicemail.

I could hardly catch my breath because just seeing him caused all the horrible memories to rush back into my mind. My therapist put me on medication for depression and anxiety, but with all that was going on right now, it wasn't helping.

I could hardly concentrate on the book I was writing, so I made a sandwich and grabbed a coke, and went to my bedroom and locked the door.

I sat on the side of the bed, my brain racing. I jumped off the bed like I was shot when the phone rang. *Could he have gotten my number?* I asked myself. Afraid it may be my husband or one of the kids, I stretched my trembling hand out and picked the phone up.

"Hello," I said, trying to keep myself calm.

"Hi Mom, how's the book going?"

With a sigh of relief, I said, "Good, really good." It was my daughter Olive. "How is your visit to West Virginia going?" I asked.

"Okay, but we all miss you Mom," Olive said.

"I miss you all too, but I need to get back to work now. I love you all... bye." I couldn't keep my voice from breaking so I had to rush off the phone.

I turned the TV on in my bedroom hoping to hear that Donnie had been captured, but soon I was fast asleep. When morning came, I was planning on writing some more, so after breakfast and a shower, I began to write. I was up to the part where I was searching for Linda. I stopped for a while to rest my eyes and stretch. As I was stretching, out of the corner of my eye I saw a set of muddy footprints inside on the carpet just in front of the glass sliding door. It looked like someone had just stood there, perhaps just watching me. The footprints were much bigger than mine, so I thought they had to belong to a man.

I was frantic now thinking that Donnie was in my house, but was wondering why there was only one set of footprints, so I stepped over the footprints and walked out on the back porch. As I looked round, I see a pair of muddy boots that looked as though they were just thrown there, far apart and lying on their sides.

Oh my God he's inside my house. My throat clogged with fear. I didn't have a hidden room here to hide like I did up Doc Polly Holler, so I ran back inside, not knowing for sure whether he was inside or outside. I ran to my bedroom where my gun was hidden just under the cover and locked the door behind me. My mind was racing and my heart thumped like an animal going crazy in an attic. I thought my heart was going to beat out of my chest, so I lay down on the bed beside my gun and listened.

I got up to call 911 when suddenly my legs were pulled out from under me. I was now on the floor once more fighting for my life, it was Donnie, the big fat monster was tearing my clothes off. I was being victimized again, but this time, in my own home. I put up a fierce fight but it didn't do any good.

"Did you miss me?" he asked with a smirk. His teeth were rotten and his breath reeked of alcohol.

I knew I had to play along or he was going to kill me, so I played along, hoping to survive. I needed to get him in the bed where my gun was. He had a gun on his side in a holster.

I told him that I missed him some, while my stomach was churning. I was about to vomit at the mere thought of him touching me.

"Let's get in the bed," hoping to get closer to my gun. Then he took his clothes off and lay beside me, then proceeded to get on top of me. As he was forcing himself inside me, I pushed him out of the bed and grabbed my gun and shot him in the leg. Blood was running from him like water running from a faucet. I immediately called 911 and reported a home invasion, and that it was Donnie Stump, and that I was one of his survivors from Doc Polly Holler, and my name was September.

CHAPTER EIGHTEEN

B ut before the police arrived, my phone rang and it was my mom calling to tell me that Detective Hollister had been killed by a drive-by-shooting. I was already devastated by what I had just endured, but now I was overwhelmed with sadness by the news about the detective that I liked very much and I was crying inconsolably.

"I have to go Mom," I told her and hung up the phone. I went out and sat on the porch to wait for the police and ambulance to arrive. Waiting on help to come seemed like an eternity. I thought he might come after me again if they didn't hurry. I didn't know if he was dead or alive at this point. Then, the police and ambulance arrived. I told them it was Donnie Stump and that my name was September. They told me they knew the case very well.

They asked me where Donnie was, and I took them into the bedroom where he lay bleeding on the floor. When they came out with the psycho, he was very much alive.

As they rolled the gurney past me, he was yelling obscene words at me and told me that he would be back. Now filled with rage, I went to push the gurney off the porch, but they stopped me.

"Don't worry September, he won't ever hurt you again," the officer said. "We're putting him in a maximum-security prison where he will spend most of his time in solitary confinement."

The CSI investigators came to collect evidence from my home including his gun and clothes from the bedroom., boots from the porch, and all other items. They were also investigating how he gained entry into my home. They took many photos and measurements throughout the house and took notes, then left.

A second ambulance came because I had to go to the hospital for another rape kit.

After they finished with me at the hospital, I went home and had to scrub myself, before my family returned. I worked until nearly dark cleaning up all the mess and then sat down to continue writing my book. I felt so relieved it was finally over.

I was up to the part where Donnie killed Annabelle. I wrote until bedtime and then took another shower. After that I went to sleep in my clean bed. There were only 2 days left before my family was going to be back. The next morning, I got ready and searched for another Psychiatrist from the phone book. I called one and made an appointment for 3pm that day.

After arriving, I had to fill out paperwork and wait for them to call my name. When they called my name, they put me in a room where I waited for at least an hour before the doctor came in.

The door opened and a man walked in and introduced himself as Dr Hampton, and extended his hand out to shake mine.

The doctor asked me a lot of questions, then I proceeded to tell him about what had happened to me and my two best friends, and what had just happened to me again at my house. It was hard to hold back the tears as I told him of the horrific things we had gone through. I told him about my nightmares and how I had multiple locks installed on my door because I was so scared. He put me on a combination of medication and wanted me to return in a week. I then headed home just to find my family had already arrived.

"Why are you guys back early?" I asked.

"I was concerned about you," my husband Derick said.

"Why?" I asked.

"We heard what happened on the news, so we came back early."

Then my husband told me I was a hero.

'Yeah, Mom you're a hero," Olive sang.

"Thank you," I said giving them hugs and kisses. "You're just in time for dinner, any help would be great," I hinted.

We fixed spaghetti and meatballs and of course garlic bread. We sat at the table and gave thanks before dinner. I explained everything to them including all the gory details. They cleaned up the dishes and went to bed so I could write some more. I continued writing until I reached the part where we received the award money then I went to bed. The following morning, the kids went back to college, and we went back to work.

It was now 1995, 2-years after returning back to work, when I got called to another crime scene where a young girl was being chased by a man. The girl reached the bridge when the man caught up to her, called her a bitch, and pushed her over. She fortunately landed in deep water.

She struggled and fought hard to survive, and knew she had to turn over onto her back and float until she could regain her breath. Passersby on the bridge saw everything and called 911. The ambulance arrived then her rescuers went into the water and brought the young girl to safety, loaded her in the ambulance, and drove away. The police were talking to the witnesses when I arrived on the scene.

"Which hospital did they take her to?" I asked. The police officer informed me that she was taken to Tampa General. Since we had witnesses that saw the whole thing, and they knew him and where he lived, I didn't have anything to process at the scene.

I decided to go to the hospital and talk to the girl. I arrived at the hospital and asked where the young girl was that was just brought in.

"Second floor room 201," the receptionist said.

"Thank you," I said and walked to the elevator and went up to the second floor. I knocked on the door of room 201. The door was open and a young girl was lying there sobbing.

"Can I come in?" I asked.

"Yes, come in," she whispered through tears.

"May I sit?" I asked.

"Of course, you can."

"My name is September and I'd like to ask you a few questions. Are you up to it?"

"Yes," she answered, "my name is Bella Clark."

"Nice to meet you. How old are you?"

"I'm fifteen."

"Can I call someone for you?"

"No, my parents are dead, and I have no family," she told me while she was drying her tears with a tissue. My heart was aching for her.

"Did he rape you?"

"No, he just chased me and then pushed me over the bridge."

"Did you know him?" I asked.

"I'm not sure, it all happened so fast, but I think he goes to the same shelter as I do sometimes." she continued, "and he called me a bitch before he shoved me over the bridge." We continued talking until the police arrived.

"Hi, I'm Detective Spencer Brody," he said as he reached out to shake her hand.

"Hello I'm Bella Clark, nice to meet you sir."

"Can you do a line up when you get discharged?" he asked.

"Yes, but only if September takes me. Will you take me September?" she asked, her body trembling.

"Of course, I will," I assured her. "I'll come back to see you every day, okay? Now you get some sleep and I'll see you tomorrow." I turned to leave the room fighting back my tears. I went to ask the doctor when she would be released.

Dr Malcolm was very kind and understanding. He told me she wasn't seriously injured, but he was going to keep her for 2 days just to observe her. I thanked him and left for home. When I entered the house, Derick was sitting on the sofa watching TV. I asked him how his day went and he said good, then I started telling him about Bella and asked him if she could stay with us for a while. Of course, he would say yes, because we both had a kind and loving heart. When it was time to discharge her, I returned to the hospital. I knew she had nowhere to go and how frightened she must be. When I entered her room, she was sitting on the bed crying.

"Do you want to go home with me for a while?" I asked. She became overwhelmed with joy and excitement. As she jumped up and embraced me so tight, I seriously had a hard time breathing.

"Okay then it is settled," I told her as my breathing improved after she let go of me. We gathered up her things and waited for her discharge papers. Finally, we left the hospital. On the way home, she asked for a hamburger and fries because she hadn't had them in a long time, so when we saw a hamburger joint, we went through the drive thru and bought enough for all of us for supper. She couldn't wait until we got home, so she gobbled up her food like she hadn't eaten for a week.

We traveled the relatively short distance home and pulled into the driveway. She only had one dirty worn-out backpack. We went inside and I introduced her to my husband Derick. They hit it off at once. Then I took her to the spare bedroom and told her she could settle in and to make herself at home.

CHAPTER NINETEEN

Bella would be sixteen-years old in a few days and we were going to have a surprise birthday party because we felt she deserved one. Derick was teaching her to drive so she could get her driver's license.

The detectives had already detained Louis Farley, age 24. We knew it would be scary for Bella to go for a line up, but I promised her that he could not see her. Hoping a party would calm her down and get her mind off things, Derick found her a nice used car for her birthday and hid it in the garage. The day before her birthday I took her shopping as she had no clothes of her own and my daughter's clothes were way too big for her.

Bella was a small little girl, 100 pounds, with beautiful red curly hair. Bella was the kind of girl everybody wished for; loving, caring, considerate of others, and always lending a hand. Since the party was a surprise, Olive, my daughter, took her to spend the night with her. After they left, we got busy with the decorations.

On the morning of her party, Bella walked in, her mouth flew open as tears dripped down onto her lips. Her beautiful green eyes were big as saucers and she was glowing with happiness. We were having a wonderful time, and after about 2 hours, my husband asked if she was ready to go get her driver's licenses and she jumped up and down with excitement.

"Okay let's go," Derick said.

"Well, are you ready?" I asked.

"Yes of course I am, let's go!" she bellowed out. We proceeded to the garage and she got there first. A car with a big bow was parked in the middle of the garage.

"Oh my God, is that for me?" she cried out in joy.

"Yes," I told her without hesitating, and with tears running down her cheeks, she ran over and opened the door, jumped in and sat down, and checked out everything inside.

"Well, we better go get that license then," Derick said. She jumped out and hugged us both then hopped into the back seat.

We drove down the road and arrived at the Department of Motor Vehicles. She passed on her first try, so we let her drive us home because it was only a short distance. When we got home, I could hear the phone ringing as we stepped inside the door. I picked up the phone and said hello.

"Hello, this is Detective Brody, we are doing the line up in the morning. Do you think you could have Bella here at 9 o'clock?"

"Yes of course," I replied, "see you then."

Bella seemed so scared and nervous, I hated this for her because she had been so happy since she came to live with us. That night, we played a few board games and went to bed. My husband and I were lying in bed discussing adopting Bella. I couldn't fall asleep, so I lay there waiting on daybreak listening to my husband snore. Finally, daylight was peering into our room. After getting dressed, I went to the kitchen and there stood Bella in an apron.

"You hungry?" she asked.

"Yes, it smells so good," I told her. The table was set and the aroma of bacon brought my husband into the kitchen, rubbing his stomach.

"Look what Bella did, and I had nothing to do with it," I said. I saw a single peach colored rose sitting in the middle of the table with a simple card that said; Thank You. After we finished eating, I asked Bella if she was ready to do the lineup.

She said that she was no longer scared and was looking forward to it.

During the short distance to the police station, we sang songs with the radio and had fun. She was ready to get this over with.

I think I was more nervous than her. As we pulled in the parking lot at the police station, she was so calm. We walked into the station and the detective was waiting for us. We followed him to a room and he shut the door. Behind the glass stood five men, each holding a card with a number on it, 1 through 5. Bella asked the detective if they could see her, and he said, "No."

Detective Brody asked her if she was ready, she said, "Hell yes, let's do this." After each man had stepped out, she told him she wasn't sure, so she asked the detective if they each could step out and say the word 'bitch'. As the third man stepped out and said 'bitch', Bella's stature changed.

"That's him," she shouted out in anger, "he tried to kill me."

"Who is he?" she asked.

"Louis Farley, 24," he replied. "Louis has been in and out of trouble for a while now and he did spend some time in the homeless shelter at the same time as you." Bella was wondering why he would want to do that to her, her mind reflecting.

"The only thing I remember was, he asked me out once but I rejected him because I was only fourteen-years old at the time. But he didn't seem to get mad," she continued.

"Don't worry honey, you are safe now," I assured her.

"You want to stop for pizza and invite Olive and Buster over?" I asked.

"Yes," that would be great, she said. We went through the drive thru at a pizza joint and bought two large pizzas then headed home. I called my kids and invited them to my house for pizza. Bella was wanting to eat the pizza before we got home because it smelled so good and we were starving. It had begun to rain and it would be the first time Bella had driven in the rain. She was driving slow as a turtle, so I asked her to pull over and let me drive until she gets more experience. As she slowed to a stop on the side of the road, a car precipitously pulled in behind us. Now we both were panicked. Because we had let Bella drive my car, my husband took the gun out of my car. We locked our doors as we watched through the rear-view mirror. It was on my mind that Bella had just picked Louis Farley out of a lineup and maybe someone was sent to get revenge. It was hard for me to stay calm in front of her, considering what I had gone through in the past.

The rain had begun to fall down in sheets and the thunder was loud and persistent as the lightning streaked across the sky. We couldn't switch seats now because a car had parked behind us. Bella was curled up in a fetal position in the back seat.

Keeping an eye on the car behind us, I searched my purse for my phone, and anything I could use as a weapon if needed. *Maybe he pulled over because of the downpour of rain,* I thought, trying to stay composed. The phone was dead and the only thing I could use as a weapon was a metal nail file.

I unexpectedly found myself holding on to Bella as she tried to open the door and bolt out of the car, but I finally persuaded her to come back up front with me and I would protect her. We switched seats quickly, then as I slowly steered back onto the road, watching to see if the car followed us, but it did not. I then noticed a missing child poster on a utility pole, so I stopped next to it and there was a picture of Bella Clark, except it wasn't the name Bella, it was Stephanie Laverty. It also had a phone number. I was very upset that I was going to adopt this girl that I assumed was a runaway.

"Why?" I asked Bella, why did you lie to me?

"Because I hate my dad," she shouted. I steered back onto the road after I wrote the phone number down and headed home. After we got home, she stormed inside the house and stomped off to her room and locked the door.

My son and daughter came for pizza just a few minutes later and asked where Bella was. I told them she was in her room, but I would explain later what happened.

I went to her room and knocked on her door, but she didn't answer, so

I assumed she was too mad to talk to me right now. I went to the garage to call the phone number I saw on the missing child poster.

My heart was breaking, but I had to call them and tell them where she was, so I called the number I had written down. A soft voice of a female answered the phone.

"Hello, this is Mary Laverty, can I help you?

My voice was quavering as I was heartbroken. "Hi my name is September; do you have a minute to talk?" I asked.

"Of course," Mrs. Laverty replied, "how can I help you?"

"Do you have a missing daughter named Stephanie? about sixteen-years old." As soon as I spoke the name, the screaming and crying began. The woman fought through her tears and started telling me about what happened and described her daughter to me.

"She is at my house and she is safe," I assured her. "I'll text you my address and you can come and get her tomorrow and we'll tell you the whole story, okay?" I texted her my address and all of a sudden, the woman said she was coming now, she couldn't wait any longer.

"I'm not that far away," she said excitedly, "so I'll see you in an hour." But before I could say another word, she had hung up. It didn't seem like an hour had gone by before she was at my door ringing my doorbell. I opened the door and welcomed her in. Her eyes were red from all the crying.

"Have a seat, and I'll go get her," I said, then left for Stephanie's room and knocked on the door. I told her that her mom was here, but no response. "Stephanie," I continued calling her name. After several attempts to get her to come out, I went back to get her mom to try and get her to come out, but we were unsuccessful. Feeling suspicious, I asked my husband to check the garage to see if her car was gone, and sure enough it was. Mrs. Laverty was visibly upset and I was trying to console her.

"She couldn't have gotten far," I told her, "she doesn't have any money and I have all the information the police need to find her, so I'll call 911."

I got Mrs. Laverty a cup of coffee and called 911. I described Stephanie and her car and gave them her license plate number.

As we were waiting on the police, I told Mrs. Laverty everything from beginning to end. I showed her all the photos we had taken of Stephanie, trying to get her mind off what was happening. My husband told us that he had gotten Stephanie's door open.

Upon entering her room, we noticed that everything was gone. I was working very hard to stay calm, I was totally heartbroken. I called her cellphone over and over but it went straight to voicemail.

"I can't believe I just found her and lost her again before I even got to see her and talk to her," Mrs. Laverty said, crying hopelessly.

CHAPTER TWENTY

At last, the police arrived, and behind them was the media swarming my house because they had learned that the girl that was pushed off the bridge, was the same girl that was reported missing from my house. As the detectives were looking around, they noticed a set of footprints just outside under Stephanie's window. It was a large footprint, so it wasn't left by Stephanie. As the detectives were investigating, the CSI investigators came and began their investigation. Mrs. Laverty and I were chatting, when she divulged to me that she was divorced and the custody battle was nasty, but she had gotten full custody of their daughter just 1-year earlier.

"Could she have met up with her dad somewhere?" I asked.

"Definitely not, she hated her dad," Mrs. Laverty said irritably, "she has run away before because of him, but never for this long."

The detectives and CSI worked tirelessly hoping to find any clue that would lead them to the whereabouts of sixteen-year-old Stephanie Laverty. After collecting what little they found, they left and the media left right behind them.

At around 9 o'clock, I asked Mrs. Laverty if she wanted to spend the night with us but she was wanting to go home in case Stephanie showed up, or if the police called. I asked her to please stay in touch and let us know if she needed anything because we loved Stephanie too. As I showed her out, she whispered softly, "Thank you all so much for helping my daughter, I promise to stay in touch."

"Okay be safe!" I said with a heavy heart. Days turned to weeks, weeks turned to months, and there was no trace of Stephanie or her car, she seemed to have disappeared off the face of the earth. My husband and I no longer felt safe here anymore and I needed to work on my book, but it was too upsetting for us to stay in Florida.

Our kids were okay with our decision to move, so we looked on the internet for houses for sale in California and wanted it to be in a gated community. We looked at many videos on realtors' websites. One house was of interest to the both of us located in San Diego, California.

It would be a 2-day trip driving, or a 5- hour trip flying.

It took a couple weeks to get everything done, but we decided to fly, and we were now on our way. It was a nice trip and we both needed to get away. We arrived in San Diego and it was absolutely beautiful with its idyllic climate, pristine beaches, and world-class family attractions and zoos, and LEGOLAND. We picked up our rental car and found a nice hotel and checked in. We were famished, so we ordered room service.

We were looking forward to seeing the house come morning. We watched a movie and ate then got ready for bed. Morning came and we got dressed and left to meet the realtor.

It was about a 2-hour trip. The road had many lanes of traffic and people were speeding up and down the highway, but thankfully we weren't on this dangerous road long before we turned off. We found the address and drove up to the guard shack and told him who we were and who we were meeting. They confirmed it was us, then let us in. The road to the house was lined with beautiful palm trees on both sides, it was breath taking. We located the house and pulled into the driveway where a lady was waiting for us. We followed her inside and looked around; it was not as big as our house in Florida, but plenty big enough.

The house was white with an open floor plan. The door was painted blue with gray shingles, with a large lot adorned with a beautiful landscape of garden lights, shrubs, and palm trees. We were impressed, so we told the lady we were interested. It would be 1997 before we sold our house in Florida and moved to California.

I worked on my book when I could because my hectic work schedule. Finally, in the year 2000, I got my book published, but was still waiting on the movie based on my book: The House up Doc Polly Holler.

Lightning Source UK Ltd.
Milton Keynes UK
UKHW012130130521
383693UK00007B/324/J